Jasmine Falling

SHEREEN MALHERBE

MB Publishing

This paperback edition published 2015

1

First published in 2015

Copyright © Shereen Malherbe 2015

Typeset in Garamond

ISBN: 151977074X
ISBN-13: 978-1519770745

Bism'Allah Ar-Rahman Ar Raheem,
First and foremost, *alhamdulillah* for all the blessings
bestowed upon me and my family and for my journey
which inspired me to write this.
Thank you to my wonderful mum for always telling me
that I can achieve whatever I want in this world ever since
I wrote my first word.
Thank you to Michele, Shumi, Vinnie and Sarah for
reading the multiple versions, and being the first ones to
fall in love with the book. Your support made it possible
to finish.
To my dad and Zuzu, thank you for taking us back to
Palestine and making us so welcome there. To the people
of Palestine, thank you for your warmth, generosity and
strength. Your stories inspired me to capture our shared
history.
My heartfelt thanks goes to my husband for the late nights,
encouragement and dedication, for being alongside me
throughout it all and by helping me turn it into what it
could be. And lastly to my beautiful boys who have spent
days typing next to me and highlighting my edits.
I love you all.

CONTENTS

CHAPTER 1

'Jasmine, she is dying.' A sharp blow to the cheek made her consciousness return for long enough to bring her surroundings into focus. She watched her mother convulse on the sofa. Their household maid, Su, turned and threw up in the sink with the phone receiver clutched in her hand. The clock ticked in the background, the dial stroked past midnight. 'Find him, Jasmine, before it is too late.'

'Who? What do you mean?' said Jasmine. Her mother stopped breathing. Frenzied adrenaline took over. Jasmine clasped her hands together and pushed down on her chest until ribs cracked. A groaning sound echoed from her mother's throat as her soul was pulled out through her mouth. 'No, mother, please. Don't leave me, I need you!' Jasmine screamed, shaking her until her mother's hair piece fell off and her waxy skin turned grey. 'Please, God help me. Don't leave me alone please.' Her sobs turned into whimpers. The clock stopped. The sky above them was an impenetrable black. The Angel of Death had blocked out every ray of light from the sky. The *Jinn* inhabited the shadows in the room, feasting on the scene.

Jasmine had hoped she would have the fortune of her mother dying in a hospital bed; her body pumped full of oxygen, her lips fat and pink, her skin rosy and her eyes closed in restful sleep. Instead, her mother's jaw had broken through its spasms and now remained motionless, her eyes fixed to the skies. When they took the body away, Jasmine remained on the sofa where it had happened. She was sedated for a week after the episode. Time passed in a melancholic blur of sombre faces and funeral rituals.

On the seventh day, sheer necessity took her away from the house. Outside, the sky was open, vast and dull. Her journey took her into the populated city of bodies. The Queen's portrait flickered in her eyes. The light speckled through the bay windows and bounced off the brass wall plaques, turning them into liquid gold. The next words she heard brought her back into the solicitor's office. 'Ms Hanson bequeaths her estate to Jasmine Elizabeth Nazheer. The sum of £7.6 million pounds will be payable in addition to the full ownership of her estate,' the solicitor paused abruptly.

'What is it?' Jasmine asked.

'Miss Nazheer, your mother has requested that the funds aren't to be released unless your father countersigns.'

'That can't be right. He's been missing in Palestine for ten years.'

'It was your mother's caveat when she wrote her Will. I am afraid without it the money will not be passed to you.'

'She was crazy,' Jasmine tried to restrain her voice, 'the same thing happened to grandma, she wasn't right towards the end.' Her eyes spun around the room trying to find someone to back her up. They fell upon Richard, her mother's closest friend. He slunk into his chair and didn't say a word. Henry took off his spectacles and squeezed the bridge of his nose with his fingers. 'Professionally, I can't get around this. Find out what you can about your father. I can fight for you if you try to find him, but if you don't, there is no guarantee-'

'Please, just stop,' Jasmine said, struggling to control her breathing. She didn't want Henry to say it out loud.

'There would be no guarantee she would receive her inheritance'. The room began to spin.

'Miss Nazheer, there is something else.' Jasmine breathed deeply. A nauseating panic twisted her organs into knots. Tears threatened her eyes. 'Before you leave you need to know what else your mother decided,' Henry took a sharp breath. 'The deadline to acquire the signature will expire in ten days from the Will reading.'

Jasmine stormed out of the office. She opened the door to her B.M.W, climbed in and shut the world out. She twisted the key so hard in the ignition it almost snapped off. Stamping on the gas, the engine roared with her as she sped off in the direction of home. Outside the windows, pedestrians in dark coloured business suits and pastel shirts blended into silhouettes and the greys shifted to shades of green. The lanes tightened to a single through way. Stones crunched underneath the car tyres as Jasmine drove down the winding private lane. The damp country air cooled her skin uncomfortably. She flexed her hand on the steering wheel and tried to shrug off the doom that crept with the cold into her neck and shoulders. The house loomed into view, unwavering against the dull sky. It consumed its plot and seemed no longer to belong where it was built. Jasmine looked away and saw the church. Its pointed spire pierced the sky. The chipped, spitting gargoyles looked down ominously, mocking her, knowing all along what was to come of the spoilt, rich girl who threw stones at them from her palace window. They watched, sat opposite her classical home built from an idea better suited to ancient Grecian tales. Jasmine's whimsical fairy-tale was beginning to crash down around her.

When she reached the privacy of her drive-way she slowed down and sobbed. The beautiful, rich life she had painted to save herself was crumbling away, replaced only with her nightmares. She had done everything to avoid going back there again. When she had composed herself enough, she got out of the car and entered the empty house. Everything about her mother's betrayal screamed at her the moment she was inside. Jasmine's figure reflected back at her from the hall mirror. Her pale face looked lost amongst the black. She would have thumped it but the strength had dissipated from her body. She traipsed down into the basement, rummaged around in the wine cellar and carried two vintage wine bottles upstairs to her mother's bedroom.

Their cleaner had been there and the room smelt washed and new. The grand, four posts on the bed stuck into the air. The swathes of torn material had been removed some time ago. The sweat patches and sick stains had been bleached away. The dresser was polished and displayed her mother's Chanel perfume collection. Standing in the centre was a photograph of two figures who had loved each other once. She smashed it to the floor along with every bottle of her mother's scent. She found the control to the stereo system and blasted the music until it temporarily filled the empty void.

She searched her mother's medicine cabinet and took a sample of the prescription drugs inside. They mixed in her blood and made her feel numb. It was a pleasant feeling that overtook the pain and left her in muted consciousness. Her body felt anaesthetised and ecstatic all at once. Jasmine spun around whilst the night fell. She barely noticed the darkness creep in.

The nights spent caring for her mother during the last eighteen months flitted in and out of her memory. For most of those she had been kept awake, shivering on the sofa in her mother's room listening to her nightmares come alive. Illness lingered in the room so she had kept the window open despite the cold, to blow the cancer out.

Now Jasmine was drawn to the same open window. The stars were absent from the sky and the dwarfed light of the moon faded in the abyss. She climbed out onto the ledge, unaware of her unsteadiness. She couldn't make out the ground below. It swirled underneath her like a

4

bottomless pit. The cold bit at her skin. She wavered at the top of the building she had called home. Now the building didn't even belong to her. She held her breath and leaned forward into the night. 'Jasmine!' A strong hand grabbed her from the ledge and pulled her back into the room. 'What are you doing girl? Are you crazy?' Richard said. Her body dropped from his arms as he lay her on her mother's bed. He pulled the windows closed and locked them.

'I don't need anyone. Especially you Richard. Go away.'

'Call me in the morning when you are feeling better.' On his way out, he called Su, 'Keep an eye on her, please. Check her breathing and if it becomes irregular call an ambulance.' Su picked up her skirt, hurried upstairs and sat by her bedside.

Jasmine awoke to Su drifting in and out of sleep in the chair. 'Am I completely ruined, Su?'

'No, of course not, Jasmine. Don't say that,' she replied, shifting herself up and wiping her eyes.

'I can feel it. There is nothing left.'

'There is good, Jasmine, inside you. When the hospital spoke to you about placing her in care, you refused.'

'Some things just don't feel right.'

'You washed her and fed her, kept her company through long, painful nights and I never heard you complain or moan.'

'What did I have to complain about? She was the one dying.'

Su released her hand and threw open the curtains. Jasmine hauled herself up. Broken memory fragments returned from the previous night. Despite the ache in her head, Jasmine knew what she had to do. Her mind cast back to the day a trunk of her father's belongings had arrived in a peculiar fashion. It had been several years after he had last been seen that a young boy had knocked at the door and asked for Mrs Nazheer. She had stood opposite him as he looked at her with his owl-like eyes. When she walked towards him, he took a few steps back.

'*Assalam Alaikom*, these are your *baba's* things from Jericho.'

Jasmine had listened to his Arabic accent with suspicion. 'Have you seen him? Do you know where he is? Did he give you this?'

The boy stammered, 'No. I... don't know.'

Jasmine grabbed him by his misshapen suit collar. 'Why are you here then? Do you think I want his junk when I haven't seen or heard from him in years?' Her hands gripped him so hard her knuckles were white. It was only when he tried to wipe away the wetness from his face that Jasmine let him go. He immediately turned and fled down the drive, her mother running down the stairs in vain. 'What did he say, Jasmine? Where has he gone?'

Jasmine booted the trunk stood at the foot of the door. Despite the pain, she ran up the stairs without another word and had never looked at it again. She had seen the basement light switched on during the years that passed. It was her mother down there, weeping. Jasmine didn't go down to her. She preferred not to think of the father she had adored and how he had left her.

Now, she knew it was time. Her feet were cold on the marble floors. She descended down into the underbelly of the house where the marble turned to concrete, illuminated by artificial light. The four walls of the basement reminded her of a mortuary. Cold slabs of stone covered all four walls, the ceiling and the floor. The journey down the steps into the third section of the basement made her heart palpitate. She switched on the light. A jumper she knew so well lay creased on the floor. She picked it up and breathed into it. The smell of burnt golden grass had long faded. She wrapped it around her shoulders and tied it across her chest. Suitcases, old frames and pieces of artwork were piled around the edges. Her mother had buried them all down there after he disappeared. They assumed he was dead but the Israeli government had refused to issue a death certificate. Still,

Jasmine's mother did her own burial in the ruins of the home they once shared. This part of the house, beneath the floorboards, became his resting place. The furniture, if uncovered, would reveal their life just as it was before he had gone. Jasmine could see the sleigh leg of the rocking chair she used to have by her bed. She imagined him sat in it whilst he told her his stories. The stories that had helped her to fall asleep, incited dreams of hot lands where mosques dominated the landscape and the call to prayer filled the air. He had always been by her side, full of knowledge about the world he had figured out.

It was obvious that this was where her mother kept the trunk as well. She spotted it, half hidden underneath a dust sheet. Jasmine went over and pulled it out. It was lighter than she expected. Her hands shook as they tried to undo the metal clasps keeping the trunk shut. She forced open the clasp so hard she broke her nail, taking off the skin from her fingertip as blood dripped from the wound. Sucking at it she sat back and opened the lid.

Inside she pulled out his prayer beads. She remembered them hanging from his wrist as his fingers counted the beads, Arabic words whispered lightly under his breath. An empty cloth bag with Arabic script written on it sat on top of a stack of letters, bound together with string and edged in a navy and white pattern. Newspaper articles, maps and missing person posters lined the base. She pulled out a few pieces and saw her father's face in one of the posters. He looked at her sideways on, behind him an orange and lemon orchard filled the background. She stared at his face. His skin and bones formed into the man she had loved once but the years had faded her memory of him. His eyes were like hers. He looked as though he belonged to a different time, an alternative life that could have been. She wrapped the photograph in paper and slid it inside his red record book he had once used. She was nervous about how to even begin searching for him. A decade had already passed since. She began to skim read the contents of the papers, her eyes desperately searching the letters that formed the words and pictures of his life.

A photograph of the Noble Sanctuary shone up at her. She had found it; the starting point. It was the place her father loved the most, the closest place to *Allah*. She would go straight to Jerusalem. She could see it now as the streets formed in her head, immersed in his stories once again, back in his forgiving land. She scooped up the pile of the letters, articles and his record book. With his prayer beads still wrapped around her wrist, she closed the trunk with a purposeful bang and walked back towards the stairs. Something slipped from her fingers. She looked down in the dim light and saw the photograph of the hyena. Captured in a moment of rage it bashed the cage, its body twisted and its teeth stained with blood. Around the cage, six men stood with home-made spears crafted from wood and sharp metal tips. A chill ran through her. She had forgotten about the hyenas. She picked up the photograph, shoved it deep into the middle of the book and left the dark behind.

That afternoon, she arranged her trip with meticulous details so not another thought could sneak its way into her mind. The plan was to head to Amman, Jordan, and then cross the land border into Palestine. Flying to Tel-Aviv was not an option considering her father's background. The Amman route was the way he would have travelled. She booked her flight to leave that evening. She pushed the nightmares aside, avoided her mother's bedroom and packed her passport in her hand luggage. Her hotel was booked and the phone call was the last thing to do. 'Hi, Richard?' she said, awkwardly.

'Jasmine? Is that you?'

'Yes. I am leaving to go to Palestine tonight.'

'I am not sure that's a good idea. You shouldn't go. No. It's definitely a bad idea.'

'I don't have much choice. You heard what the solicitor said.'

'How will you even begin to look for him?'

'I have some idea of where to start and I will see where that leads me.'

'It doesn't sound like a very good plan but can you be convinced otherwise?'

'No. I never believed I would say this but, I am going back.'

She felt his annoyance in the long pause before he said, 'Should I look after the house for you whilst you are gone?' Jasmine agreed, hung up the phone and went upstairs. The door to her mother's room was open, willing her to go inside. It was difficult to remember what she had been like before the cancer. The illness had stretched on for so long most of the threads of their life before had disintegrated, but if Jasmine pressed her eyes shut, she could sometimes clutch the fading memories before they disappeared.

The cup and saucer on the bedside table stirred her. When the world was dark and silent, she would quietly find her mother's favourite coffee cup amongst the stacked dishes. She would giggle to herself at the irony of tiptoeing around when her sole purpose was to rouse her from sleep. She would measure the fresh coffee and boil water in an old metal pot with a long handle. Jasmine often looked for one to replace the old fashioned, scarred one but her mother insisted that no other pot could make coffee like it, so she had stopped looking. She would add sugar and simmer it down until the smell of roasted coffee beans and cardamom sweetened underneath her nose. As she brought it to her bedside, her mother's eyes would open and flash a knowing smile, her pink bow lips raising her cheekbones high into her face, listening to Jasmine spilling out that nights dramas. When the birds outside tweeted a warning that dawn was about to arrive, Jasmine would panic at a night of lost sleep and climb in next to her mother, drifting off to the comforting aroma that circled the room. It melted away her troubles and the sound of her mother's breathing soothed her to a rhythmic sleep as if she was a new-born again.

The day she told her about the illness was vivid still as was the betrayal that she could let it happen. Her childish dramas became replaced with a harsher reality. The warm, safe memories were gradually chiselled into sharper, uglier ones. The coffee left her mother retching into her sick bowl. Her sleep was random and disturbed. When Jasmine lay next to her mother at night she didn't recognise the short breaths or the smell of sickness and bleach. Her cheekbones stuck through her cheeks like daggers and the colour from her skin had drained leaving her white-washed in the moonlight. When Jasmine was sure she was asleep, she would turn off the bedside lamp that her mother refused to switch off. Jasmine had been warned about the side effects but they hadn't told her she would scream not to be left alone in the dark. This bothered Jasmine the most, the fear creeping under her skin and burying itself there.

Jasmine heard Su come into the room. She waited patiently by the door with her eyes fixed on the suitcase. 'Where are you going, Jasmine?'

'I am going to find my father in Palestine.'

'Are you sure?'

'If there is a slight chance that I may find him, then I have to take it. I have left him for too long already.'

'Oh, Jasmine, I wish you didn't have to. I'll worry about you too much.'

'I have left details with Henry, should anything happen to me.'

'Please, don't,' Su mumbled through stifled tears.

'I have told him to take care of you. You and your son will have everything you need for your future. Don't waste your feelings worrying about me, Su. Please give Richard a spare key whilst I am gone.' Su nodded but her face turned away. 'Get the house ready to be sold. Take everything off the walls and arrange it for it to be sent to storage.'

'What about her clothes, her things?'

'All of it. I want it all gone.'

Jasmine picked up her suitcase and walked out of the bedroom. Tears pricked in her eyes but never fell. She concentrated on moving forward, struggled down the stairs and outside to await the taxi. The cold air numbed her face. She saw the taxi lights approach on the driveway. As the taxi pulled off, she turned back to look at the house, watching it shrink away into the distance until it disappeared for good.

CHAPTER 2

Jasmine arrived in Amman just as an amber sunrise cracked through the horizon. The trip left her body reeling, dehydrated and sick from withdrawal. She drank to avoid the worst of it but the foreboding feeling sat in her stomach throughout the whole journey, intensified by the black night time air swirling around outside the plane's window. The stars died and the clouds turned into pools of grey, hanging like waiting ghosts. She passed through the airport terminal and booked a taxi to take her straight to the land crossing into Palestine.

The taxi wound through deep-cut mountains. Thin streams and herds of goats tackled the steep, uneven land. 'Not far now,' said the taxi driver in a thick accent. The landscape flattened out as banana plantations, dilapidated streets and shops made of concrete filled her vision. Mechanic garages had piles of rubber tyres outside and the slick of dirty engine oil seemed to coat all the walls, the Arabic signs outside and the pavement it sprawled out on to. People milled about on the streets in conversation and young men sat on upturned oil drums in well-worn jeans with cigarettes hanging from their mouths. As the taxi approached the imposing grey gates of the border, the shops turned to car rental agencies littered with old cars for rent and beggars waiting to pounce on the next tourist. 'You need to go there,' said the taxi driver as he pointed in the direction of the gates. 'Ok. Thanks.' She paid him, took out her luggage and instantly regretted the heaviness of her suitcase as she rolled it along the uneven road.

The visa hall sat behind a driveway lined with coaches and taxis. The air was flat. When she walked in, people stared. Jasmine sat down in her expensive linens, her silk blouse and untarnished travelling sandals. She noticed she was the only solo female in the crowded room. Women wore *abaya*s and didn't seem to mind the flies resting on their veils as their harem of children ran around, unaffected by the heat. Men with full beards and robes sat next to others in tired suits. A cranky fan twisted on the side of the wall. In the centre of the room, stood glass booths. Jasmine went over when her number was called. 'I need a visa to Palestine.'

The visa guard looked at her surprised, 'You are Palestinian?'

'And British,' said Jasmine.

'Board the coach outside,' he said, stamping paperwork and counting out change in a series of notes. 'The next one leaves within the hour,' he gave her a friendly smile. 'Have a good trip.'

No one had said have a good trip before, she was used to warnings instead. It was the main reason she hadn't gone back. Years ago she had thought of returning, she had begged her mother to take her. Her mother's response was gentle at first, she said if he came home he wouldn't find anyone there. That made sense when Jasmine was a child but as the years passed by it wasn't good enough. So her mother told her tales of random shootings, security lockdowns, high partition walls and a hostile army which soon scared any idea of it out of her head.

She climbed on the coach and walked down the aisle. She watched as mothers preened their children, wiped their noses and aimed hand held fans at their red cheeks. As she sat down, she wondered how a mother could betray their own child. Memories of her own mother and her grandmother came flooding back. Jasmine was the next in line to have her sanity disintegrate. The thought made her shudder. Her perceived susceptibility to disease was heightened ever since she watched her mother die. Her heart beat strongly underneath her skin, the pulsation made her feel sick and she couldn't rid her body of the parasitical feeling that coursed in her blood.

The coach doors moaned. She glanced around and noticed that she sat next to the only spare seat. She looked out of the window as the coach started along the bumpy road. In the distance stood concrete watch-towers manned with armed soldiers. Security fences wrapped around the perimeter, topped with ferocious looking tangles of barbed wire. The coach was slightly cooler than outside but the air was tinged with apprehension. Jasmine could hear breaths and whispers. The children were peculiarly quiet now.

The coach pulled in and stalled next to a drab military checkpoint. She watched as three guards approached and boarded the coach. The coach engine went dead. The driver walked off. The guards were now only a few seats in front of her. She heard the children stifle their sobs. 'Passports,' they said, as a hand was held out at her.

Jasmine stared in disbelief. She stood her ground. 'I am British,' she said. One of them turned and shouted in Arabic to the armed officer standing at the door who nodded in return. 'You come with us,' he said as they grabbed her by the arm.

'You're hurting me. Get your hands off me!' Jasmine struggled. Her arm felt like a bird's wing trapped in a lion's mouth. The other passengers sat in silence. Everybody watched but no-one moved. 'Doesn't anyone care where he is taking me?' A veiled woman on the seat nearest to the door whispered something familiar in Arabic. Just as

Jasmine tried to turn to her, she stumbled and tripped down the steps, landing face down in the dirt. The guards brought her to her feet. She spat out gravelly sand as they led her inside the blacked out building. She heard the engine of the coach restart and the tyres crackle on the gravel.

'What are you doing here?' said a man sat opposite her, half hidden by an old computer screen. His uniform was pinned closed where his hand should have been. 'I am here to visit family,' said Jasmine. A hand on her shoulder forced her to sit down.

'Why do you travel alone? Where is your mother?'

'In a grave, back in England.'

His face remained blank. He spat tobacco ends from his cigar on the floor, 'Your father?'

'Missing,' said Jasmine. She sensed a change in his demeanour. He moved his face from behind the screen and stood looking her up and down. 'Look, I don't have long. I need to see my family in Palestine and then I will go back home.' The armed man who had taken her off the coach was finishing a phone call in the other room. He walked over to the officer and they spoke in Arabic. 'It seems that you have been here before.'

'I have been once before. It was a very long time ago.' A grey haired man with a collar length beard came out from the back room. He wore badges on his lapels and walked with authority. 'Leave me alone with her a minute,' he said, holding her passport. When the others had left, he continued, 'What is your father's name?'

'Ibrahim,' Jasmine said.

'I know your family name Miss Nazheer, I apologise for this situation,' he said, sitting himself down on the chair and leaning back with a heavy sigh. 'We will take you to your family. We know them well. I presume you will go to Jericho only?'

'Yes,' Jasmine said. 'My uncle has a farm there.' He shouted in Arabic. A shabbily dressed man attended them.

He listened to the instructions and opened a side door revealing a desert coloured, blacked out SUV parked outside. 'I am not getting in that,' said Jasmine.

'It is that way, or back home. You choose?' he said, handing her back her passport. He held the door open until she climbed inside. When he had disappeared from view, Jasmine told the driver to take her to Jerusalem instead. 'No, no, Miss. Jericho.'

'No driver, Jerusalem. We will be driving around Jericho all night. Just take me there and I will pay you good money, Ok? You understand? Five hundred *Sheikl*, you take me to Jerusalem.' He looked annoyed but didn't say anything else or reach for the radio. Jasmine smiled. Everyone had their price.

The SUV barely made it out of the dirt tracks surrounding the borders. The driver manhandled the wheel as it heaved and fell with scrapes and bumps until eventually reaching a road. She was relieved to be on smooth terrain and to see another car at last. They approached the coastline. A sign pointed to Jerusalem, but they drove straight past it. 'Is this the way to Jerusalem? We just missed the turning,' Jasmine queried, fumbling around in her bag trying to find a map. The driver responded in Arabic, raising his hands in annoyance. The Dead Sea appeared on their left, looking more like a pearlescent lake than a sea. Dried up salt crystallised around its edges, giving the illusion of washed up jewels glistening on its banks. The car slowed down. She looked up to see commotion ahead on the road. Battered trucks blocked the road. As the car stopped she climbed out to take a closer look. Men with rifles hanging from their shoulders argued with drivers queued at the roadblock. Behind her the engine backfired. Other men waiting in the back of one of the trucks jumped out and bolted towards her. The driver reversed, smashed his back bumper on a boulder and sped down the road leaving her alone. The armed men fired two rounds after him then left him to it as they muttered indiscriminately. They spotted Jasmine and jogged towards her, weighted down by their rifles. She didn't move. 'Who are you? What are you doing here?' They said, in coarse English.

'I'm Jasmine, I...'

'She's with me,' a man's voice said from behind them. He thrust himself between them and turned to face her, 'We are travelling through the old towns on route to Jerusalem to see the Holy City. You have wanted to visit for a long time haven't you?' Jasmine nodded blankly and forced a smile. Gunshots fired in the distance. Nodding briefly, they retreated with the rest of their militia back to their trucks and sped off. The other queued cars slowly pulled off now the road was clear. 'Thanks,' said Jasmine.

'No problem, is this your first time here?'

'Not exactly. It has been a while.'

'I thought so.'

'Sorry but who are you?' she said, now fully noticing the young guy standing next to her looking smug.

'I'm Josh,' Jasmine didn't say anything so he carried on, 'There aren't many tourists that visit here, what with the trouble, so you kind of stand out. And it looks like you might need a ride somewhere?'

'Yes, it looks like I do,' she said.

Her beating heart reminded her she was alive. The sun barely broke through and the sea retreated in his presence. Jasmine could see his strength, she could hear it in the deepness of his breath and see it in the tautness of his body beneath his shirt. Josh beamed at her and graciously opened the door to his Jeep. She climbed inside. 'Where are you staying in Jerusalem?'

Jasmine pulled out her travel plans. 'The King David Hotel.'

'You chose a bit of a detour then?'

Jasmine shrugged. 'Do you know where the hotel is?'

'I know everything about my city,' said Josh.

After an hour, they approached Jerusalem. The city

made her feel claustrophobic. It was segregated by checkpoints and around its perimeter, soldiers stood guard. A winding wall at least eight metres high cut up the city. Barb wire sat atop the grey exposed concrete face, towering above Jerusalem as it coiled itself around like a hideous snake, entwining through and dividing neighbourhoods. Defiant graffiti stained it with declarations of freedom. 'What is that?' said Jasmine. 'It's a security fence,' he replied.

'Who are they trying to keep out, King Kong?'

Josh laughed nervously, 'Not quite.'

'It looks like the Berlin wall to me.' They slowed as they approached the queue of cars waiting at the checkpoints entering Jerusalem. Local Palestinians queued inside the roadside barriers that led to the Wall's crossing. They were herded through the gun-metal grey barriers. A group of school children were pushed back in line, each one labelled a potential security threat, their small bodies searched after passing through scanners. A soldier ripped off the rucksack of a young boy, throwing it to the floor as he pushed him up against the barrier to search him again. Incensed, Jasmine swung open the door and jumped out. 'Hey, you can't do that!' she shouted at the guards. She threw herself in front of the boy and pushed him to safety. The soldier shouted at her and grabbed his rifle around his shoulder. The boy pushed back in between her and the soldier, then turned to face her and said, 'I am Ok, lady. I'm Ok.' His young features were worn but defiant and fearless. He grabbed his rucksack off the guard and walked through the cattle gates, disappearing on the other side of the Wall.

'What are you doing Jasmine? Get back in the car now.' Josh easily pulled her back into the car as if she weighed nothing and slammed the door. 'You can't do that.'

'Why not? They can't treat a child like that. What's wrong with you?'

Josh held his breath whilst the soldiers searched the car

at the checkpoint. Armed guards watched them suspiciously as they checked the chassis with mirrors. A nod from the guard gave them the all clear. At last they were waved through into the centre of Jerusalem.

CHAPTER 3 JOSH PART 1

His eyes scanned the roadblock up ahead. Six uniformed men armed with M16 rifles and fingers poised over triggers stood offset from each other, some arguing with the driver of the first car as the others watched. The roadside barriers had been lined up in haste and out of line providing an effective enough barrier to stop the traffic. Behind him, a female tourist left her car. He watched the passengers in the other cars. He found it odd that they barely noticed her. Josh thought they would have had they breathed the moment she passed. She had turned the wind sweet.

The sun had fallen low in the sky and dusk was threatening the horizon. Shadows had grown behind the boulders that were scattered around the Dead Sea, ground away by the continuous lull of the waves which slowly tortured its shoreline. The sea rippled in the slight breeze and sparkled like thousands of silver butterflies falling on its surface. As he stared, her presence dulled the sea into a monotonous swathe of navy, cutting a light silhouette on the backdrop. She walked past him, her dark hair tumbling around her shoulders. Even in the failing light, Josh could see the creaminess of her skin and the pale strawberries peaked in her cheekbones. The way her flesh and skin shaped around her, he had seen beautiful creatures before but never one this extraordinary. She possessed a light inside her, flickering like a slow burning candle.

Josh turned around sharply. Her driver had reversed hard, smashed into a boulder and careered off. He faced the armed men, apprehension rocked through their limbs. Radios crackled with no response. She stopped dead as they charged towards her. Her nostrils flared ever so slightly as she rapidly took in more air. He noticed her fingers fiddling with a ring on her right hand, twisting it around so many times it must have marked her delicate skin. But she stayed firm. Her back was straight in defiance and her eyes unwaveringly met theirs. An electric shiver shot through his body.

Within seconds he had positioned himself between them. The situation was diffused. Gunshots fired in the distance. The men's speakers buzzed with erratic voices. They ran back to their trucks and sped away. The queue dispersed, allowing them to pass.

They eased into their journey together as the roads widened and her story unfolded. Whispers of her father floated through the air and pricked his skin as though they weren't meant for his ears. She had visited before, but that wouldn't help. It was too many years ago to be of use. The place was beyond recognition now. He had never struggled to read a person, but she evaded him. Her strength was not an act to hide her vulnerability, it emanated from inside of her and seemed to disregard her own self-preservation. It had thrown him completely when she leapt from the car at the Jerusalem checkpoint.

Now, the streets were clear and the world quickened around them. He slipped his number into her bag as she stepped from the car. Disappearing into the hotel, he stayed just long enough to see her glance back. He drove off and parked up a few roads away to wait. Within an hour he had received the message. He started the engine and sped up the hilly side roads which made up the old part of the city. The narrow streets were lined with brick walls, encasing the Jeep on both sides. Hundred-year-old stone houses sat behind the walls with flat roofs overlooking the Noble Sanctuary. The roads twisted higher until the Dome of the Rock glinted in the moonlight below. Figures on top of the roof courtyards curved into chairs as they watched the night engulf the city. He moved quickly between them until he arrived at a remote part of the city. The neighbourhood showed signs of irreparable damage and the homes were uninhabitable. He climbed out of his Jeep and slipped off down a winding street that blended into the ruins. There, in the grey light, the city was blocked from view. Even the starlight was dulled. The figure stepped from the shadows as if born from the *Jinn*. Josh walked forward and handed him a note.

'You have been busy. What is your plan?' he said to Josh.

'I don't have one,' replied Josh.

'That is a first for you.'

'I mean; I am working on it.'

There was a pause, long enough to impart his unhappiness. 'I will see what can be done but surely I don't need to remind you?'

'Of what?' Josh said, playing the game. He knew what was coming next.

'We aren't part of the same world. You don't need to be reminded of the consequence of what that means.'

Josh nodded in automatic agreement as they parted. He spent the rest of the night and early hours of the morning drowning in a pool of vivid dreams. A fire raged in his blood. The phone rang. Her voice cooled the flames and soothed his anguish. He was long past adhering to a constrained set of rules, even if they had been established before his country was even born.

He pulled on a hooded jumper despite the warm weather. He yanked up his hood, grabbed some belongings and headed out the back door. He drove his Jeep through the city, backtracking down side streets and watching to see if the shadows passed behind him in his rear view mirror. The day was too bright to hide anything. The sun bore down on him from its closest point to the earth. He briefly longed for the coolness of the night air and the breeze it carried with it as he parked in a secluded spot, under a canopy of mature trees planted between the Old City walls.

CHAPTER 4

Jasmine woke up in the strange room far from home. She climbed out of the hotel bed with the blanket draped around her shoulders. She shuffled over to the curtains, pulled them aside and peered outside for her first peek of the Holy City. The rising dawn light cast an imposing shadow across the Old City walls. Its dark cloak protected its secrets. The duty of trying to find her father amidst it all made her groan. She stumbled back into bed. The warmth from her blankets lulled her to rest. In the midst of sleep and wakefulness she saw the maze of winding streets and high walls that built up the Old City, partly made up from her memory but with guarded secrets seemingly impossible to extract. Her father's stories that once richly painted her childhood had cracked and flaked. They were nothing more than the swirling dust in a crumbling city.

She dreamed of coffins and earth. She watched from above at the lump of soil, under which her mother lay. She looked through the soil, her eyes penetrating through the heavy lid of the coffin. Her mother's body squirmed in the blackness within the gold lined coffin, made not with an exuberant solid gold but fool's gold; a cheap trick played upon her soul for which she was now paying the price.

Jasmine awoke with her heart aching. Her head flitted between the bed and the grave. She reached out to stroke the fabric of the sheets but somehow it seemed to feel like soil beneath her fingertips. With the dawn light in her window and her head clouded, sleep was not a possibility. She pulled out the pile of her father's things and un-wrapped the white string from the letters. They had no postal address or stamps on the front.

Dear Papa,
Winter, 1935
I am sad you missed my twelfth birthday. Roxana spent most of the day crying. She says it was her fault you were taken because you saved her. They took you instead. I told her you are the strongest man I know and if you haven't escaped already, that you soon would. I have seen it in my comic books, where the heroes plot their route, scale electric fences and escape from the bad guys. I told her they will be no match for you.
I am still attending school each day despite the soldiers. I found the book you hid. I have started to read it so the pages are as familiar to me as they are to you. I often place it in your chair and imagine you reading it there, just like you always did. I will not return it to the library. The library was burned down last week so no one will miss it. The book is ours.
Yours, Bert.

Jasmine had no idea who Bert was. She was sure she hadn't heard the name before. She put the letter aside and decided to find something to wear so she could get on with her day. She had no idea what the weather was going to be like, so she switched on the television. The news told her how the world had changed whilst she slept. She remembered Josh. Suddenly, dressing became more important. She looked at her reflection in the mirror. Her hair was knotted at the back where she had rolled around in her nightmares. Her mascara was embedded into the creases below her cheeks and her lips were dry from the

25

mid-flight drinking. She wondered how she would pass the morning. She went through the pile of papers again. A phone number, with Josh's name scribbled on, floated down above the pile. She smiled, before shaking it off her face and returning to the task in hand. A local Imam from the Noble Sanctuary had featured in an article about government archaeologists digging under the grounds there. Her father had recorded his concerns; the dates and times when it started and the precise location of the excavation areas. There in black and white was a record that the Imam had spoken to her father. Perhaps they had known each other well, she mused. Maybe the Imam could tell her something that would lead her to him.

After her shower she stared at the clothes, most of which had the labels still on, heaped on her suitcase. She hung most of them in the wardrobe and left a pile of her favourites on the bed. She would have to choose something that didn't look as if she had tried too hard. She also didn't want to stand out, it had to be suitable for the Noble Sanctuary. She eventually decided on a navy maxi dress, paired with a silk patterned jacket and a scarf that could be wrapped over her hair or around her shoulders in case she was still out in the evening. She imagined that if she would be out in the evening, it might be with Josh. She picked up the hotel phone and her hand became damp on the receiver. Her breath heavy, she took two deep gulps of air and punched in the numbers with her fingertips. It rang once. *'What am I doing?'* It rang again. *'Put the phone down'.*

'Hello.'

'Hi, it's Jasmine, we met yesterday,' she said, rushing out the words. He didn't reply. The silence made her cringe. She glanced at the clock, it was early still. She wondered if hanging up now would make the situation better or worse. She figured worse. 'Near the road block, you said you could help if I needed it.'

'Of course I know who it is. Is everything Ok?'

'Yes, sorry. It's just I wondered if you could show me

around today?'

The pause seemed to stretch on uncomfortably before Josh spoke, 'I'll meet you in the Christian Quarter at midday.'

Jasmine hung up. She couldn't bring herself to say anything else. She didn't want to waffle on like she did when she was nervous and make herself look even crazier. *'Crazy like her grandmother, crazy like her mother.'* She brushed the thought from her mind. Today, she had hope still. She was in the land of her father and whatever his story was, she could deal with. This time she had her fortune waiting for her and it would help to build the life she had dreamt of. With spare time before she met Josh, she picked up the next letter from the stack and went downstairs to breakfast.

Dear Papa,

Spring, 1935

Things grew worse since you left. We don't go to school anymore. The teachers and our old friends act strange with us. The teachers measure our faces and our old friends kick us in the playground. Mother left some weeks ago to go into hospital. I stayed with Roxana and her family in their wagon pulled by strong horses.

One morning I had a nightmare about never finding you, so I left them sleeping and wandered out into the field with their mare, Diamond, for company. When I returned, they were all gone. A metallic smell lingered in the air. Roxana's doll was left behind with its head ripped from her body. Since their disappearance I have roamed the fields and woods with Diamond for company.

I don't want you to worry though, papa. I can catch rabbits. I don't have the means to make a fire so I tear their fur from their flesh and eat them raw. The taste isn't as bad as you would imagine. They are warm and leave me full.

Dusk scares me. The plain clothes men come into the town. I have begun to notice how they walk. It is different to everyone else. They walk like army men. When it gets too cold I sleep next to Diamond. Sometimes I listen to her heartbeat when I feel I have forgotten what life sounds like.

I am devising a plan to escape these days and nights, it is a plan we used to speak about when we all shared the same bed in the warmth of the bakery. I will dream of it tonight. And there I know, from the bones in my body, I will find you.

Yours, Bert.

With nothing else keeping her in the hotel she left and started the walk to the Old City of Jerusalem. She had seen its old Ottoman-era walls from her room and knew it wasn't far. From the streets, the gates of the Old City loomed in to view. They towered above her with locks clamped on either side of the open doors. A raven squawked from a perch on its walls, the sound splintering through her bones as she entered into the maze. Smoke hissed and escaped from kebab shops, shisha smoke blew from the lips of old men, drawn from decorated glass bulbs. Tourists walked aimlessly, dazed by the sounds and smells of the bustling market. The shops were made of the same mould, cut from ancient stone and formed from the natural concaves in the rock. Merchants hollering from their stalls selling brass camels, pure woollen rugs stitched in traditional patterns, woven dresses and glittering jewellery. Arabic inspired décor, wooden carvings of the nativity scene, crosses and figures of the crucifixion were in abundance ready for the next dazed tourist to buy. The place itself felt familiar. It had barely changed in thousands of years despite the wars, crusades and occupations. A feeling of Deja vu crept into her bones, reminding her of the nightmares she used to have all those years ago as a child. Being back there had reminded her of the old Jasmine. The sound of sellers shouting and tempting her to go inside their shops, to look at the stalls and buy gifts cluttered her head once more.

She walked towards the centre of the souk where the Noble Sanctuary stood. It was the place her memory had let her hold onto from her childhood. Various entrances led into the courtyard. The narrow, uneven cobbled streets tightened and the bustle disappeared. A cat purred close to her ankle, smelling of dank earth. Soldiers stood outside the entrance to the Noble Sanctuary. A young soldier fixed on her and approached with the crunch of heavy boots on the gravel. The cat slipped into a gutter and darted off. '*Assalam Alaikom*. Is it Ok to go through?' Jasmine asked.

He nodded his head as he looked her over and gestured her through. Calmness seemed to overtake her emotions. Fruit trees and manicured lawns adorned the pathways. It opened up into a square courtyard that she knew to be the most holy site in Jerusalem. She pictured her father standing there. The Dome of the Rock with its Persian blue tiles and gold topped dome glimmering in the bright sunlight. She heard her father's voice tell her again the story of the night Prophet Mohammed was visited by Angel Gabriel as he slept in Mecca. Angel Gabriel's six hundred wings, embellished with rubies and emeralds, had stretched and filled up the sky from the East to the West. Prophet Mohammed had journeyed with the Angel on a winged horse to where Jasmine was standing now. Together they had prayed with the re-awoken past prophets at Al Aqsa mosque, bowing before the Almighty in the last third of the night when He was closest to earth. Before the white thread of dawn reappeared, the winged horse flew them back to Mecca, just as *Allah* ascended to above the heavens and the sun rose from the sea. *'Don't forget your heritage here, Jasmine. Don't forget the lands heritage. It is part of you.'* Her father's voice resonated in her head. It cut through her until she forced it into the back part of her mind where the remnants of her past lay buried.

A man dressed in a white robe, wearing a traditional black and white chequered headscarf stood some distance behind her. '*Assalam alaikom*,' he said.

'*Wa alaikom salam.*' She hadn't forgotten everything. Her accent must have been good as he replied to her in Arabic. 'Sorry, I speak English. Little Arabic.'

'Ok. My English is fine. You are lost?'

'No. I am searching for something.'

'Yes, I see. You haven't found it yet.'

'I meant, someone. I am looking for someone.'

Jasmine recognised the man's face from her father's documents. She dug around in her bag and pulled out the article. The Imam peered over it. 'That was written some years ago.'

'I know. It is just my father; he documented the excavations around the Noble Sanctuary. He kept a record here,' she said, showing him the pages of dates, times and collections.

'Ibrahim, he was a good man,' he looked at her. 'So you are his daughter?'

'Yes, yes, I am,' said Jasmine feeling the hope desperately seep out into her vocal chords.

'I am sorry. I cannot help you. I don't know what happened to him. We tried, we all did but...' His voice trailed off. Jasmine could tell he didn't want to say anything else, a religious man did not add to the gossip.

'Is there anything you can tell me about where I might find him?'

'Perhaps only *Allah* knows, Miss Nazheer. Maybe you should ask him to help. *Insha'Allah* you will find what you are searching for. *Assalam Alaikom*'. He turned slowly and left.

'*Wa alaikom salam*,' Jasmine whispered. She watched him enter Al Aqsa mosque. A few minutes later his voice rang out from the minarets filling the entire city with the call to prayer.

Back in the bustle of the souk, Josh stood waiting for her in the square of the Christian Quarter. It was a small square of sandy rock coloured buildings with churches built into the edges around it. Their wooden arch doors were wide open, beckoning the tourists inside. 'That is the Church of the Holy Sepulchre. Christians believe Jesus is buried there. They also believe it is the site of his resurrection and the place he will return to,' said Josh.

'And what do others say?' Jasmine said sarcastically, not expecting a reply.

'Well, it depends how far you go back. In the Roman times, in the early second century, the church was a temple to the Roman Goddess Aphrodite. Others believe it was a temple for Venus although most believe that is made up.'

'How is it that you know everything?'

'Well, I studied it. I majored in History and specialised in the Middle East.'

'That explains a lot,' Jasmine laughed.

'Do you want to go inside?'

Jasmine shrugged. 'I may as well whilst I'm here.'

There was no denying the church's presence once inside, completely defying its modest and ancient exterior. Intimidating oil paintings lit with solemn faces stared down at her. She spun around and came face to face with a stone statue looking through her with fixed eyes. Josh stopped her at one of the gilded alters. It dripped with silver and gold adornments, painted figures and candlesticks. 'Underneath the glass here,' said Josh as he knelt down at the altar, 'is the Golgotha. The skull shape rock on which crucifixions would take place.'

'So that's where Jesus died?'

Josh's voice turned to a whisper, 'Jasmine, he wasn't crucified. Why do you think he was seen later? The logical explanation is that he never died in the first place.' She walked away from it, rubbing the goose bumps which raised her skin. Tourists prostrated themselves on the floor, kissing and worshipping the figures. Her father's voice was there again, resonating from the old walls. '*Haram,*' he would say sternly as Jasmine's young eyes watched the same unfold years ago. *'To imagine that the Almighty Himself can see them kneeling at carvings of stone.'* She looked into the shadows of the church at the unseen *Jinn* laughing at those figures prostrating to stone. 'What are you looking at?' Josh asked.

Jasmine shook her head. She had forgotten about the tales of the *Jinn* that her father warned her about. Now, being here the memories were returning like a slow and purposeful spider. With its long, black legs the nightmares would creep into her mind each time she closed her eyes. Then, she would see through the creature's murky eyes. She would see the carcass of a deer as it lay in the glistening white. She would watch the hyena tearing at its sweated flesh, blood seeping into the snow forming warm pools of death around her feet. And in that moment, the deer shifted. It shifted into the shape of a young boy.

It was the *Jinn* her father had told her, when she was young enough for him to stay but hadn't reached the age where he had abandoned her. They are the shape-shifters *Allah* created from the smokeless fire, sent upon earth to try to tempt the transgressors away from the true path. The path of the righteous and the only path to heaven. Jasmine had heard it many times before. Each time she had a nightmare or was ill after playing out at night, he would remind her. He warned her they were invisible to human eyes, but they would be there, tempting her whenever weakness fell upon her. She could protect herself he said, and with that he would speak in the tongue of the heavens. His lips would curl around the words and sound from his throat as he recited the Holy Quran. The only protection Jasmine could have in this world were His words, he said. Then she would imagine the *Jinn* not as huge impenetrable figures that could steal her away in the night, but as whimpering cowards who disappeared into smoke. This new awareness would remind her of the Angels in all their magnificent beauty and enormous stature. Even in the heavens the Angels, with all their purity, would tremble at the sound of God's voice. *'Don't you forget that Jasmine,'* her father said. *'If the Angels tremble, then we mortals must never forget to fear Him.'* But Jasmine had forgotten.

'Let me show you his tomb,' said Josh. Jasmine didn't

want to see the tomb. Her childhood stories, the burning candles, the images depicted on the walls all pointed to the same warning. Their eyes stared to the depths of hell beneath the floors reminding her she was unable to escape from it. Her breath shortened. Sweat beads started to crawl down the side of her forehead. Heat started to rise from her heart and consumed her flesh. The crowds seemed to close in and steal the oxygen from around her. Then she saw him amongst the crowds and voices and backpacks. 'Father?' she tried to shout but her voice barely managed a whisper, 'Wait!'

***

She opened her eyes to the shade in the cover of the church. Josh dampened the bottom of his T-shirt and pressed it onto her head. 'Jasmine, you were mumbling about your father.'

'I saw him Josh. He was in there.'

'You can't have. You fainted. I had to bring you outside.'

'No. I saw him, Josh. I did.'

'Alright. We will go back inside and have another look but stay close to me.'

'No, I don't want to go back inside. We will watch from here. Everybody has to come out right?' Josh nodded. He hovered about her, touching her cheeks with the back of his hand and feeling the pulse in her wrist with his forefinger. 'I will go and get you something sweet to drink. Maybe it's the humidity. You aren't used to it.' Josh jogged off to the nearest shop. She believed her thought process to be entirely rational. If her father was inside, he had to leave or someone else would have seen him. She hung around the bottom of the steps and weakly showed his picture to the people that passed her by. The same sympathetic responses rolled on, one after another. 'We all see ghosts inside there.'

'Maybe you need a break? Come on. I will show you some other parts of the city. Take you for lunch?' Josh said, as they drank down the sweet melon juice.

'No. I am not hungry.'

'I will just wait until you faint again then, shall I?' Jasmine managed a smile. They walked out of the courtyard and into the tight winding streets and alleyways. She was like a magpie, drawn to the shop windows whenever something glinted. She would wander in and Josh would almost lose her. It was late afternoon and getting busy. He held her arm as they dodged people and overtook slow walkers who seemed content on getting no-where fast. 'Where is this place?' said Jasmine, but Josh didn't hear her above the bustle of the different languages, bellows of the traders and the clanging of brass pots in kitchen shops. She lent closer and repeated it into his ear, feeling his skin brush her lips. She liked being so close to his face. His skin was warm and slightly bristled from his rush to meet her this morning. She liked the idea of that. *'He rushed to see her.'*

He took her by the hand and tucked her hair behind her ear. Her skin tingled. 'I know a short cut,' said Josh. His hand was strong and firm. He effortlessly weaved them through until the streets quietened and the shops were slowly replaced by populated houses hidden behind old brick walls with clean laundry hung on wrought iron Juliet balconies. Jasmine looked up at the plants and screens on the rooftops of the piled houses. She imagined living there in the middle of it all, walking home and climbing the uneven stairs in the ancient city, sleeping when the streets were silent and the places of worship were empty. She imagined people washing their clothes in big, metal tubs and sleeping on wooden cots on the sparse floors after a modest meal, eaten on the rooftops whilst they watched the sun sink over the Holy City and told stories to their children. Similar to the stories her father once told her, but with the setting in front of them. From their roofs she could have seen Salahaddin and his men fighting the battle for the city, the flash of their swords and the neighing of the horses as they bucked and galloped under their riders, loyal and fierce.

Jasmine brought her eyes back down from the roof terrace and noticed an orphanage with a flaking painted blue sign and gates barricading the door. 'Come with me,' said Josh as he led her down a small side alley. They ducked down behind a low brick wall. Beyond the wall, girls in blue pinafore dresses and boys in navy shorts and shirts played in a courtyard. They played hopscotch and kicked balls as the sounds reminiscent of her school playground carried into Jasmine's ears. Memories of school days, where strife and dreams of the future mixed together with the untainted optimism of youth, made her smile.

Jasmine turned down the next path, following Josh. The air changed. Heavy tarpaulins above their heads blocked out the sun. Surrounding her were slabs of flesh and the chopping sound of meat cleavers chomping through bone. The nausea was back rising inside her stomach. She yanked her hand free of Josh and ran until it was far enough behind her, that the smell had gone and the hacking was almost inaudible. 'Are you Ok?' asked Josh, catching up with her.

'I am a vegetarian. That was probably my worst nightmare.' She couldn't help but laugh.

'Lunch?'

She winced. Her sprint meant they had to turn down a few more streets before they arrived. It looked the same as all the other fast food and falafel kiosks, but the smell brought with it familiarity.

It had been a rain soaked day back at the house before her father left. She was sat, crossed legged on the carpet drawing shapes in the condensation that formed on the patio windows. The trees lined the length of the garden, curving around the manicured lawn. They were old trees with tough barks and they hung low with the burden of the persistent rainfall, sending sycamore leaves whirling to the ground like falling helicopters. An unusual smell had wafted from the kitchen. Jasmine looked up at her mother on the sofa who peered over her magazine, a wide expression lit up her eyes, feigning surprise. 'Your father must be cooking.'

He was surrounded by a heap of used pots piled by the sink, the oven was on and open, dough was lumped on the side, the blender was filled with a green paste. He turned to her amidst the mess. 'So, you want to see how the chef does it? Come on, I will teach you some things.' He lifted her on to the side and showed his ingredients, 'This here is falafel paste. You grind boiled chick peas and add heaps of parsley and garlic. This is the dough for the flat bread. My mother taught me how to make all of this.'

'And you eat this for breakfast?' she said.

'We eat falafel all the time. Breakfast, lunch and dinner back home, but I love it for breakfast.' She liked watching him and imagined him cooking in the far away country he was born from. 'What is it like in Tata's kitchen father? Is it like this one?'

He spun away from the oven with the heat from it in his cheeks. 'No, Jasmine darling, nothing like our kitchen.'

'Tell me what it is like.'

'She has four rooms in the whole house.'

'Only four!'

'Yes, four rooms. The kitchen is about the size of our oven. It has one sink, four gas rings attached to a big gas cylinder about as big as you and cotton curtains over the units for cupboards.'

'Wow, it sounds so different.'

'But you would love it there. The farm Jasmine, it has everything you can think of, lemon trees, orange trees, we grow mint, parsley, coriander. There are chickens clucking all over the place.'

'Real lemon and orange trees? You can eat them?'

'What else do you do with lemons and oranges? And

not just lemons like we get here, huge lemons the size of grapefruit,' her father had replied cupping his hands around an imaginary fruit more the size of a watermelon than a grapefruit. Jasmine laughed. Together they worked the green paste into golf sized balls and dropped them into the deep fryer. They sizzled until they smelt toasty and when he lifted them out they were golden brown. He then rested the falafel on hastily piled kitchen roll and went over to the dough. 'You can help with this if you like? We are going to make flat bread just like your Tata.' He handed Jasmine a small lump of dough. She rolled and smacked it with her fists as her father laughed. 'Gently, Jasmine, you need to do it gently,' he said, slowing down his voice and working the dough. 'There, that's better. Now it's ready to roll out.' Together they rolled it out into balls, flattening them with the rolling pin, placing them on the heated baking tray as they went. Her father pushed the tray into the hot oven and closed the door. Jasmine's mother appeared, propped up against the kitchen door, 'Looks like you two are having fun!'

'Mother, mother, we made falafel and flat bread just how Tata makes it. Have you seen the lemon trees in the gardens there? Can you really pick them off and just eat them?'

'Yes, Jasmine, you can.'

'Wow. I want to go. Can I?' Both of them fell quiet and Jasmine's mother looked at her father.

'Maybe when you are a bit older.'

'I think it is a wonderful idea,' her father replied.

'It isn't as easy as that.' Her mother's voice tried to be light-hearted.

'I will keep her safe.'

Her mother sighed, 'Ok, we will talk about it another time. It smells like breakfast is ready.'

Jasmine whispered to her father, 'Please take me. I want to go.'

'And *Insha'Allah* you will, Jasmine. It is as much a part

of you as it is me.' Jasmine remembered that as the moment she fell in love. The foreign land was now a part of her, her own slice of her father's home filled the English walls and was theirs for the whole morning.

'Hello. Are you still with me?' said Josh, 'It is the best falafel in all of Jerusalem.' Jasmine looked at him as she gazed at the lemons and oranges piled up in the baskets. They chose a table that faced the main walkway and above it, bright parasols shaded them. Josh brought a tray over with hot falafel sandwiches, Arabic dips and salads in paper bowls. They both faced outwards and tucked into lunch. She was hungrier than she realised and the food was delicious, maybe even better than her father's. 'Where will you look next, Jasmine?' She liked how he said her name. It made it sound beautiful.

'I don't know. There is a place he wrote about in his book, a place where locals went to look for their missing loved ones.'

Josh stopped eating. 'I think I know where.'

'Really?'

'I did tell you this is my city.'

'Where is it?'

Josh leaned in closer so no one could over hear. 'We are standing above it,' he said, pointing to the floor. Jasmine screwed up her eyebrows. He shifted even closer to her until she felt his breath on her cheek and his knee against her leg, 'I think it is in the caves.' Goosebumps tickled every inch of her skin. 'Will you take me?'

'Of course I will. There are many stories of missing people being found under Jerusalem. Underneath us, is a network of old caves. Historically it was hiding place, a bunker that provided secret escape routes.'

'It's getting late, I'm not sure going at night is a good idea?'

'It is full of tour guides and tourists during the day. We wouldn't get a chance to look where we need to go. It's our only choice if you want to rule it out and move on?'

Jasmine glared a little. Josh knew exactly what to say to make going there the only option. She wanted to find all the logical reasons in the world to avoid the underground, especially at night, but none came.

As dusk began to fall, Jasmine reluctantly followed him around the exterior walls of the Old City. They were protected from the street by leafy trees which blocked them from view. The public entrance was locked shut. Josh pulled out his Swiss army knife and forced the lock open loudly. He paused to make sure no one had heard

'We shouldn't be here,' whispered Jasmine.

'I know. Just don't let them catch you.'

'Who?'

But Josh didn't answer. He had already slipped into the mouth of the cave.

CHAPTER 5

Inside the caves, grey rock rolled around them, rising and falling in natural formations, opening to form a wide auditorium with carvings etched into its walls. Lanterns lit up the space. Drops of water fell like tears from above. He explained the caves themselves were rediscovered in the 18th Century after five hundred years of being sealed off for fear of transgressors entering underneath the holy ground. The caves stretched to the Prophet Jesus' tomb and wound through the length of the city. He told the story of the fox that had howled every night at the concealed entrance to the caves, only to disappear whenever dawn threatened to break. One night, a man called Herod happened to be awoken by the fox's cry. Herod went to where the howl had come from to find damaged stone. He chipped away where the fox had scraped. It was then he discovered the caves mouth, opening up into a network complete with the skeletons of those who had died centuries before.

Josh led Jasmine deeper into the caves and pressed a finger against his lips. Holding her hand, he pushed a section of the cave wall. It parted slightly so their bodies could slide sideways through the gap. Inside, a hallway lit with torches partly revealed the depths. 'To the real tombs,' Josh whispered. Jasmine shivered. She stayed closed and gripped his arm. She took a few seconds to enjoy the warmth of him against her body and sought comfort from it. The tombs almost airless passage made it hard to breathe. Josh took a candle from the floor, lighting it from the wall mounted torches. Ahead, the passage way opened up. Under an arch, a stone tomb lay elevated on a rock bed. An intricately carved figure of a man lay with his hands crossed over his chest. She saw his bearded face with carved eyes that stared past the cave ceiling to the heavens. Josh pulled her through another gap hidden in a crevice behind the tomb. Her eyes swam amongst the shadows that danced from the candlelight. Above her, a staircase made of stone spiralled upwards. They climbed the stairwell and as they reached the top, a slight breeze flickered the candle flame. Josh pressed up against the rock wall. 'All clear,' he said as he pushed it firmly. Once again, a seemingly immovable rock shifted, revealing a chamber.

Missing posters covered the walls of the cavernous space. Jasmine studied the many faces in the prime of their life, distorted by the dampness that had forced them to disintegrate. 'What is this place?' Jasmine whispered.

'I am not exactly sure but I heard that the missing turn up here sometimes.' Jasmine added a poster of her father to the wall. They wandered further into the cave blindly with no natural light but the candle, followed by their shadows as they cast themselves awkwardly onto the walls. As they moved further inwards the cave closed in. It twisted and turned. Smashed pieces of crockery and aqueducts lined the route. 'This is where people used to hide when the city was being attacked during the old battles. They set it up pretty well with access to fresh water that trickles into here collected from rain pools all over the city, there are sections for keeping livestock and cooking equipment,' Josh said, pointing out the various fragments of old artefacts.

'Where does it lead to?'

'Where does everything in this city lead to?' he whispered in her ear. 'To the Holy Ground.' Josh moved away from her and pressed on, picking up broken pieces of crockery, disappearing and reappearing down enclaves and passages. Jasmine's heart dropped each time he wandered from her view. She looked around trying to find a way out. The walls wrapped around her. Her chest tightened. She tried to control her breathing and in panic tripped and fell, dropping the candle to the floor, leaving her in complete darkness. 'Josh?' She felt around to recover the candle but couldn't find it. Standing up, she felt for the wall, following it guided only by her hands. 'Josh?' Her strained voice echoed through the passage. Her heart began to pound and her lungs closed in. 'Josh,' she shouted this time, 'where are you?'

She felt the matchbox in her pocket and tried to light a flame. Her hands shook and forced her to drop the first match on the floor, then the second. On the third she struck. A ball of fire lit the dark passage for a few seconds. Two figures moved in the darkness. Jasmine turned and ran. She stumbled and picked herself up again. Running blind, she hit the wall. Pain pounded through her forehead as she collapsed.

It was dark outside in the snow. The cold bit into her skin. She wasn't alone but she couldn't make out the others. A child's cry was carried through the wind. Jasmine could sense they needed her but she was paralysed. She tried to call out so they knew they weren't alone in the darkness. No sound left her lips. Ahead of her, a hyena circled around a carcass, staining the snow.

Jasmine opened her eyes. She winced. Torchlight made the back of her pupil's ache. The light shifted to the side. She was sat in a chair in the middle of an opening. The security guard with the flashlight spoke. 'What are you doing down here?'

'I was lost,' Jasmine replied.

'What are you looking for?' She didn't answer. 'We will call the police you know.'

'I am looking for someone. Someone who is missing. I was…I was told to look here.' Saying it out loud made her feel stupid.

'You were not alone?' Jasmine wasn't sure if it was a question or not so she didn't say anything. 'What is your name?'

'Jasmine. Jasmine Nazheer.'

'Wait there.' The guard doing all the talking left, another sat a few metres away. He glanced at her occasionally, then went back to chewing his nails. After ten minutes the other guard returned with someone else. He was in plain clothes, about fifty years old with a long beard. 'Come with me,' he said. Jasmine stood and up and took a few seconds to get her balance. She touched her forehead where the pain was coming from and felt a sticky cut. She followed his torchlight. 'I believe you Miss Nazheer. Who came with you?'

'I was with a…' Jasmine paused. 'A friend.'

'And how long have you known this friend?'

'A couple of days.' Jasmine followed him as he weaved through the passageways effortlessly, as if they were signposted.

'I know your family name, Nazheer, but you do not belong here sneaking about underneath the holy ground. Your name will not protect you from others.'

'You know my family? I am looking for my father.'

'There is no reason your father would be buried underneath the city. It is nothing but story-telling and misguidance. Ask *Allah* to guide you and if it is His will, you will find him,' he said arriving at an opening within the wall where the fragrance of jasmine and the night-time air wafted in, reminding her of her mother. 'I have tried looking but I don't know where to start.'

'Maybe you are looking at it wrong. You are looking for

something, but perhaps you haven't found what exactly you are looking for.' He beckoned to the opening and stood silently until Jasmine went outside. She began to walk off and then dashed back. 'Wait!'

She heard her voice echo inside the cave. A sharp voice hissed back, 'Try the fairground.'

Jasmine followed the street lights to a more populous part of the city until she was comforted by the late night revellers buzzing around her. The sound of music and the sight of steamy bar windows pulled her inside to what she knew best. She drank to numb the stinging in her head and, one after another the sweet liquor made it disappear.

It was a few hours later when she stumbled into the hotel. She attempted to walk up the stairs to get to her room. 'Jasmine!' A voice shouted from behind her. She turned around to see Josh in the lobby. He ran up to her. 'Oh God, I am so sorry. Are you Ok? I am so sorry.'

'What happened to you? Where did you go?' she said.

'I followed the trail of the aqueducts. Some I had never seen before, they were new I'm sure of it and they lead to new passages.' Jasmine frowned so Josh quickly got to the point. 'When I turned round I couldn't see you anywhere. I was so worried.'

'Ok, it's fine,' Jasmine said, rubbing her head. The throb reminded her of what he had left her to.

'Let me see,' he said parting her dishevelled hair.

'No, no it's fine.'

'I won't be so careless with you again.' He dusted the soil from her sleeves and wiped a smudge of mud from her neck. Unwittingly, her lips smiled. 'What is it?' he said.

'Nothing, I'm just not used to it.' She didn't explain anymore and probably wouldn't have even said that if she wasn't tipsy. He nodded and looked at his watch.

'Come on, we better get you to bed, it's late.' His face turned red. 'No I didn't mean like that. I mean to your room, alone.'

'I know.' Jasmine laughed. He held his hand

protectively behind her and led her up the staircase to her room. When she closed the door, he checked the handle twice to make sure she had locked it. She watched him through the spy glass and saw him pace the hall for a few seconds before he disappeared down the stairs. Jasmine retreated to her bed. A pile of letters crinkled underneath her. Pulling them out, she leaned into the lamp light to read.

Dear Papa,
Summer, 1935
One night, while passing the bakery, I saw a candle flicker from the window. I had heard about the homeless vagrants occupying the empty country houses from the towns so I didn't dare to go inside. I dared not to hope it was her. But mama had come back for me. She brought your new daughter, Liora with her. She is the essence of light, papa and she looks just like you with her fair curls and bright eyes. I adore her already.

The evening reminded me of one of the nights before you left. I am sure you will remember. The night mama made sweet apple pie and we stayed up all night playing games with the radio turned off. You allowed me to fall asleep on your lap on the sofa. If only I had known then it would have been one of our last for a while, I would have forced myself to stay awake to spend more time with you. I wasted it with sleep.

I told mama of the plan to leave, to be reunited with you soon. I will write again when I know more. I will take care of them until we are with you.
Yours, Bert.

Getting up, she raided the mini bar, hoping to find something to relieve the returning throb in her head. She pulled out a bottle of Pinot and poured it into a glass, inhaling the smell of berries and alcohol, reminding her of her English mansion.

Most nights she had pulled a few bottles from the basement. When her mother rested for long enough for her to escape out of the room, she would tiptoe to the basement and fumble around in the dark. She didn't want to switch on the light and let the household know she was down there again. Once her hand felt the cork, she would move it down and wrap it around the bottle neck, tucking it up into her gown as she tottered up the stairs to the kitchen. Mostly, she would swill it around in an open jug allowing it to breathe. Other times she uncorked it so quickly it broke off into the wine bottle and she glugged it from the neck hoping the warmth would take over and provide her with some comfort. 'Come here please, Jasmine,' her mother had said late one night in her then rare moments of clarity. Jasmine pretended she was already asleep under the covers of the sofa in her mother's bedroom. 'I know you are awake, Jasmine, even with your concoctions you are a light sleeper.' Jasmine's temperature rose until she was burning underneath the covers. She threw them off and walked to her mother's bed. There her mother was, smiling, *'Ill, but still well enough to be an irritation.'*

'Lay here with me.'

'I need to get some sleep, mother. I will see you in the morning.' Jasmine left to head to her room, switching off the light as she went.

'No!' her mother had screeched, 'Leave it on.' After that, Jasmine gave in and collapsed on the couch breathing deeply but getting nothing but lungsful of stagnant air. Later, she heard her mother mutter, 'They are coming for me Jasmine, they are always watching. Now they have got in, they must have sneaked in through the window. You opened it, didn't you?' Jasmine froze. She barely breathed. Her mother didn't care if she had a response, she carried on regardless. 'They are the ones making me weak so I give in. But I won't. I know the truth. They keep telling me it's too late but I know it isn't.'

Jasmine had heard her talk that way before. Her midnight whining never made sense. It was as though her voice and consciousness didn't belong to her anymore. She had mentioned it to the nurse. 'It is just the drugs your mother is on. They are very strong, but hopefully they will make her feel better,' the nurse had replied.

'But the same thing happened to my grandmother, just before she passed. She went a little crazy.'

'It may feel strange but there isn't anything wrong with her mind. Can I help you with anything? This is a very difficult time for you.' Jasmine felt as if the nurse was fishing to see if there was any sign of her slipping into the same hereditary mental deterioration.

'No. I am fine,' Jasmine had snapped at her. She was far from fine but she had never dared to ask her about it again.

She swigged the hotel wine in one go, opening up a new bottle as soon as it had finished. Kneeling down at her suitcase, she flung out the rest of her clothes and found the medical bag at the bottom. She opened it up and pulled out the aspirin and sleeping pills. She swallowed the pills with a mouthful of wine, trying to mute the relentless tap-tapping of mental illness at the back of her skull.

CHAPTER 6

Jasmine rolled over, glancing at the letters scattered over the bed. The morning light was attempting to sneak into her room through the thick curtains. She switched on the lamp and immersed herself into someone else's world.

Dear Papa,
Winter, 1939

It has been years since I wrote to you. Liora is already four. We crossed the border into Czechoslovakia. We spent many days hiding there, I was mistaken to think we would be safer there than back in Germany. Still, it meant we were closer to our goal, to you.

An old widow found us hiding in a church on the outskirts of one of the villages. She took us in to her home and hid us in the basement. We didn't see much of her, except when she would deliver food she had scraped together. I think she fed us for Liora's sake more than ours. She asked mother if she could take Liora. Mother refused.

We would have starved to death if that was our only food, so when it was quiet enough for me to do so, I wore one of the old lady's musty fur pelts and went hunting in the woods. The trees to the woods lined the widow's garden. I relished the freedom to roam around again and breathe in the fresh air, even though the bitterness of the cold stung my throat. I hunt well now, papa.

After many weeks of hunting, the widow caught me and banned me from going outside. I had to stay in the basement. We didn't leave for weeks. My legs cramped from the lack of exercise and our stomach's from the lack of food. I longed to leave. I started to wonder if braving the cold was a better fortune than our current existence. But, I would look at Liora. Mama knew it too; she wouldn't last the outside in the harsh winter. I had to stay, for her.

By night, I sketched out our next move with chalk on the stone floor. We would leave this basement home and head onto Bratislava. Mother spoke to an old friend of yours from Germany. He gave us the name of an underground worker who helps to smuggle refugees out of Europe. I tried to imagine what this hero looked like. I said his name over and over again so I wouldn't forget what it was. For those fleeting moments, we imagined it together. The basement had been left behind. Carried by the winds, we sailed across the ocean and I saw us all together again, toiling the fertile fields in our new home. I have learned the path we have to take. The cold months are ending and we are preparing ourselves to leave.

Yours, Bert.

Dear Papa,
Spring, 1940

It did not go to plan. I write again now I am in a state to recount what happened. It was a typical sunless Wednesday morning when the widow left to go into town. She was late back so I crept upstairs and looked out of the window. I saw the soldiers in an open truck driving at speed towards the house. I knew they were coming for us. Mother screamed at us to run, so I grabbed the widow's fur pelts and ran towards the trees with Liora. They were so close I could see the melting crystals on the frosted leaves of the trees. I could hear boots chopping through the frozen grass, getting closer and closer to us no matter how fast and hard I ran. Shots rang out. Liora fell at my side. I held her hand until it slipped free. I heard mother scream. A single shot fired. I careered into the trees at such speed that I buckled, fell down a steep embankment and didn't wake until morning.

I had no choice but to go as far away as I could from the widow's house. I don't know if I will ever forgive myself for leaving. I don't know how to ask you to forgive me.

Yours, Bert.

Jasmine sighed. It had not been what she was expecting. Nothing seemed to help. She hadn't seen anything else like it in her father's belongings. She racked her brain but was sure he had never told her this story. Her phone rang. 'Hi Jasmine. It's Josh. Did you have any plans for this morning?'

'No, not yet,' said Jasmine, knowing none would materialise either.

'Do you fancy a quick trip? I have something for you.' Jasmine couldn't resist. She looked around as she put the phone down. Her hotel room looked like a pit. Clothes were strewn all over the place. Bert's letters littered her bed and wine bottles lay empty on the floor. She opened the curtains wide and winced at the sunlight. She looked in the mirror. *'Oh dear.'* She scrambled around and shoved her belongings into her suitcase. She threw the loose bits of paper in the drawer by the side of the bed and rushed to the bathroom. Josh wouldn't be long.

When he arrived, they decided to go on foot to the souk. The hotel was close and it would have been hard to find a car parking space nearer to the city. Robed men strolled to the mosque, tourists looked at maps pinned to trees and families sat on blankets outside Jerusalem's walls with picnic spreads laid out in front of them. They walked through the main gates beckoning them inside. Jasmine recognised some of the streets, the souk now had a familiar feeling. Since she had experienced it again, her memory of it was returning. Skulking around in its underbelly made her feel as though she had unearthed half of the secrets it was trying to hide; the others wouldn't be too far away. She remembered her mother's words, *'Secrets always find a way to come to light.'* Josh stopped outside an antique door sandwiched between two larger shops. 'Do you mind waiting here a minute?'

'No,' said Jasmine. She paced up and down three or four shops either side until the curiosity became unbearable. She peered through the small window next to the door. Odd pieces of gold and brass, unusual rocks and stones glittered beneath warm spotlights. Josh turned and saw her squinting through the glass. She cringed, hearing a laugh filter out through the gap in the door. She walked away and busied herself in the shop opposite, a jumble of odd bits and intriguing antiquities. She stroked smooth brass pots and felt the handmade weave of the Persian-styled rugs that were heaped on top of an antique looking chair. She picked up a delicate ceramic pot that fit snuggly into the palm of her hand. It was hand painted with flowers and a tiny humming bird. She turned it upside down to look at the price, her mother would love this piece. It fell from her hands as the past came to present, smashing into pieces as it hit the stone floor. The shop keeper came over. He stood with his hands on his hips, staring down, as if debating to himself whether or not he could put it back together. He glanced up at her. 'Don't worry, Miss-no sad- no need.'

'No, I am fine. I am sorry, here,' she said, stuffing money into his hand. She knew it was more than enough to pay for it. She wanted to get out and away from the broken pieces. Outside Josh was waiting. 'Are you Ok?'

Jasmine nodded. 'Have you finished?'

'Yes, come on I want to show you something.' They found a courtyard where the streets opened up to reveal a hexagonal-shaped fountain. The water sprayed out forming a crystal umbrella. They sat on its ledge and Josh pulled out a box. Jasmine looked at him and hoped he hadn't notice the pink flush warming her cheeks.

'I don't want this to be strange or anything,' Josh laughed putting her at ease, 'it isn't like I am going to propose, just yet. It's just this is too perfect for you, that I couldn't have you leave without it.' Jasmine opened the box. Inside, a stone clasped to a gold ring glinted like a pearlescent sea, more captivating than any pearl even though it reminded her of one. She took the ring out of the box and looked at it closely then, slipping it onto her middle finger, realised it was too small. She moved it to her wedding finger, then quickly switched to her right hand as she kept her gaze fixed on it unwaveringly.

'Do you like it?'

'It is beautiful. What is it?'

'It is another one of Jerusalem's underground secrets. Centuries ago, a stone was found that scientists hadn't seen anywhere else in the world. It was made up of the ancient earth of the city. Its wars, its stories, its hope all buried underneath layers of sand. With time they compressed and formed this precious stone.'

'It must be priceless!'

'It is, but not because of its sale worth. Not many people know about it. I discovered it whilst completing my dissertation at Uni. It turns out that because it doesn't sparkle like commercial gems it was soon forgotten.'

'That is an amazing story. Is it true?'

Josh laughed, 'You should know by now, all of the stories here are true. That's why everyone always fights over this place.' Jasmine put the box in her pocket and kept the ring on her finger. She looked at it again, liking the feeling of it on her hand. It felt secure on her finger. A sign that someone had thought of her, that Josh had thought of her. She kept repeating it to herself in her head as they strolled around the city. The city that she was making new stories in, a city whose history she had grown up with and now a history that she wore on her finger.

They spent the rest of the day together. Josh introduced Jasmine to the sights she had missed out on the previous day, with tourist leaflets stuffed under their arms and her snapping photographs of everywhere they went. The spectre of her father would appear as they crossed busy crowds, or when she saw the shimmer of amber prayer beads dangling from someone's hand. She looked deeper, but each time Josh pulled her away with more information and more sites until it became just the two of them in the city. When dusk fell, they dined in a traditional restaurant outside the Old City walls. They strolled out onto the street, content and quiet. A fairground poster floated in the wind and settled at their feet. Josh scooped down to pick it up. 'Do you fancy going to the fairground tonight?' Jasmine nodded although she suspected her reasons for going were different to Josh. The evening was cooler than she had expected. The walk was longer too. They came across the patch of land the fairground occupied. Plastic rainbow coloured lights flashed from stalls of furry stuffed animals and goldfish bowls. Chimed rehashes of old songs chimed from all around them, couples walked hand in hand across the worn out patches of grass and teenagers screamed from bucket seats spinning them seemingly uncontrolled into the night-time sky.

Jasmine wandered around the edge of the striped stalls and drank from one of the Chardonnay bottles she had taken from the mini bar earlier that morning. She kept it hidden from Josh, but when he looked at her, it was as though he knew. The plastic lights began to shine like bright stars and as the colours of the fairground dazzled, she could no longer see the crudely exposed wires running between the stalls or the dead goldfishes floating in the bowls. 'Back in the caves, someone told me to come here,' she said. Josh looked puzzled.

'Are you sure? You did bang your head pretty hard,' he said revealing the bruise on her head. 'What are you expecting to find here?'

'I don't know yet.' They meandered through the maze of tricks and treats. They shot targets for prizes, lost themselves in the giddiness of the rides and rested on the Ferris-wheel when Jasmine became too dizzy to walk. It carried them higher into the sky, away from the deluge of noise. From the caged bars she looked out onto candy stalls and face painters. A star-covered tent on the outskirts of the field caught her attention. Excitement tingled in her fingertips, images of fortune tellers, crystal balls and the ever tempting glimpse into the future decorated her eyes. The Ferris-wheel was suspended at its highest point and the impatience inside her surged. She leaned over the bars. 'Hello down there you little people! Let me off!' Josh pulled her back in.

'What are you doing?'

'I want to get off!'

'You have to wait. What are you going to do, jump?'

Jasmine sat down, looking out to the darkness and remembered how it had engulfed her the night she received the news. The fear had gone again, the fall intrigued her. It pulled her towards it with an unrestrainable force. She wanted it. She wanted to fall, to feel her body experience its limitations. She stood up on the seat and turned to look at Josh. His hand reached for hers. She pressed her head into the cold bars, wondering how many times she would be saved before she actually let herself go. All the while, her hand stayed in his.

When their carriage returned to earth, Josh helped Jasmine out. His mobile phone rang so, excusing himself and walking off to escape the noise, Jasmine found herself alone. She headed to the tent where a sign reading, *'Fortune Teller'* was staked into the ground. She pulled the swathes of material aside and followed a fabric lined entrance into the den where the space was lit by candles flickering from the floor. A dark round table squatted in the centre of the room. Jasmine hesitated and turned on her heels to leave, when a voice beckoned her back. 'Come, sit. You are here for a reason.' An older woman with thinning black hair and dirty smudges staining her eyes stood at the other end of the tent. The fortune teller pointed to the chair. 'I, I don't usually come to these things,' said Jasmine slowly, sitting rigidly, waiting for the moment to run.

'Of course you don't my dear. So are you going to let me help you? Tell me, why are you here?'

'I am looking for someone. Someone who has been missing for a long time.'

The fortune teller took Jasmine's hand and studied it in silence. 'This is your lifeline,' she said, showing her the line flowing from right to left on her palm.

'It doesn't look very long,' said Jasmine.

The fortune teller said nothing, as if she was listening to another conversation. After a few uneasy moments, she said, 'You have lost someone close to you. You feel betrayed.' Jasmine knew how these things worked and didn't answer. 'That is the real reason you are here. It is because of her.' The fortune teller paused again. 'So, the person you are looking for. Are they a stranger to you?' Jasmine shrugged. She didn't know how to answer, he felt like a stranger but it was still her father. Resentment had filled all the places left behind when he abandoned her. The nightmares had started soon after his disappearance. *'Not a great legacy to have from your father.'*

'You dream of things you don't understand but they hold the clue to where he is,' she said.

'That doesn't make any sense. I don't even know where I am in them. I have never been there before.'

'You do know; you just won't allow yourself to go there again. But once you do, you will find what you are looking for.' Jasmine had had enough. The way the fortune teller spoke reminded her of her mother's last days. She had been reduced to speaking in riddles, refusing to sleep alone and panicking in the darkness. Jasmine would spend nights uncomfortably listening to her sleep talking with the shadows and the darkness closing in on her. It scared her to think about it again. She preferred the more detached feeling she had held onto since the Will was read. It provided the cool hard facts she could cling on to; her mother didn't want her cared for, she wanted her to struggle. There was no other reason why she would deny

Jasmine her rightful inheritance. 'There is someone near you who you should be wary of. He speaks to the shadows.'

'Ok, I'm off now,' said Jasmine, throwing down money on the table.

'Wait, please. You need to hear what else I have seen.' Her words were ringing in Jasmine's ears, she needed to escape. She surged forward desperate for space as she felt her chest constrict. She hit the fresh night-time-air and strode purposefully until she reached the low swung rope that separated the fairground from the rest of the city. She climbed over and kept going until she reached the centre of the unused patch of land adjacent. She lay down on the floor and stared at the sky, covered by its magnitude and silence. The silence was broken as footsteps sounded from behind her. Her body froze.

'Jasmine, what are you doing?' You can't just wander off by yourself. It just isn't safe.'

'I needed space. That fortune teller got to me.'

'What do you expect from money makers and scam artists? That's all you'll find at the fairground.'

Jasmine calmed as he spoke. A star shot across the sky leaving a trail of silver against the black. 'Wow, it's beautiful,' said Jasmine.

'Not just beautiful, but deadly,' he said, looking up.

'Why deadly?'

'It is said that the stars are the lanterns of heaven. The *Jinn* eavesdrop at the first heaven which spreads out above the stars, stealing whispers from the Angels as they talk; they take one piece of truth, then mix it with a thousand lies. So the stars shoot across the sky to knock the *Jinn* from the heavens.'

Jasmine stared above and watched as a glimmer of gas-blue heat flickered in the distance. 'BANG!' The noise hammered through the air like thunder. Jasmine turned to see a flare of orange light. Then, the fairground crowds erupted into screams of panic. Shadows fled from where the light splintered the sky. 'Jasmine, quickly, we have to go. Now!' Josh grabbed her hand as they ran deep into the blackness of the field. She heard footsteps thudding from behind them. 'What was that?' gasped Jasmine.

'Gunshots.' Josh leapt a low wall in one bound. Jasmine stumbled over it. They crouched down on the other side. A main road showed hope of escape. He grabbed her as they darted across, almost colliding with a taxi. 'Get in,' said Josh, opening the door and looking behind him as though the danger was still imminent. They fell into the back seat, out of breath. The taxi driver looked at them suspiciously in the rear view mirror. 'I don't want any trouble, Ok? Where are you going?' he asked.

'Take us to a bar,' Jasmine answered, 'I need a drink.' Josh directed the driver to a busy street. He paid him, helped Jasmine out of the car and towards a bar on the corner of the street. The windows were covered with old music posters and smoke. Inside, regulars sat drinking in booths, with dim lights illuminating the bar and tables lit with candles in old jars that doubled up as ashtrays. They sat by themselves in a booth next to a window that, if cleaned, may have given them a view onto the street. A waiter brought the drinks over and Jasmine relaxed.

'Where to next?' he asked.

'I think I will choose the next bar. You didn't do a good job with this one.'

Josh looked around, smiled and winked at her. 'So, where was your father born?'

'Jericho.'

'Why don't you go there?'

Jasmine shifted uncomfortably. Jerusalem wasn't exposing any more of its secrets to her. A sense of dread stirred inside her. She remained silent so he excused himself and when he had left her sight, Jasmine finally allowed the echoes of her past to return. The memory was so vivid it removed her away from the crowded bar and made her temperature rise, just as it had done all those years ago.

The fever had come on quickly and left her delirious. She tossed and turned on the bed underneath itchy, fleece blankets. Mosquitoes buzzed about her ears, leaving irritating sores on the exposed parts of skin. Her Tata came in and out, wrapped in a thin floral headscarf and a long, mismatching floral dress that fell from her neck to her ankles. She stayed with her each time she came and held her down with her hand pressed on her head. Jasmine knew the Arabic words she spoke as her father had said them often, *'In the name of the Lord oft forgiving, most merciful, I seek refuge in you from the evils of the Devil.'* The words circled around her, sometimes followed by strange faces. Her father never came. Nightfall brought with it a foreboding heaviness that weighed on her head, like the feeling before an impending thunderstorm. It would ache and swell under the pressure and then the clouds would open and the release came. Only the release never came. The light turning to dark outside the hole in the wall told her two days had come and gone.

When she was able to sit up, they propped her up in bed just enough place a tray over her legs. In it, meat and bones floated in the pale yellow liquid with thin shards of broken pasta. She didn't want to eat it but the spoon was brought to her lips and the hot liquid was poured down her throat, lumps and all. When her body had recovered enough she swung her legs from the bed. She was unaware of what the time was, but she wanted to go. She imagined the airport, the promise of her English home. The plane that would return her to her mother, to her own bed, to her home instead of being trapped between the blotchy, crumbling walls unable to speak to or understand anyone. She walked out of the archway where a door should have been, into a corridor where the two rooms of the house broke off. It was empty except for a fridge and a dining table pushed against the wall and a stack of chairs piled up on top of it. The main door that led outside into the courtyard was just in front of her. Figures moved amongst the courtyard, sparks of fire shot from hot coals, seared animal flesh filled the hot air. The street ahead was dead. The houses opposite seemed derelict, their courtyards empty and closed with heavy gates. The thought hit her with ferocity as she fell to the ground. *'There's no escape.'*

Her father came back a couple of mornings later when she had recovered. She slapped him across the face, pushed past him and went outside. He followed. 'Your uncle thought now you are feeling better…he has a gift to cheer you up.' The farmer's old donkey was tied outside. He lived down the road but he lent the donkey to Jasmine's uncle whenever he needed to take produce into town for market day. The donkeys still had right of way on the roads and were allowed into the souks before the cars.

The donkey rubbed his nose against the low, stone wall outside the farmhouse. It grunted and kicked its feet on the ground trying to get free from the rope. Above the grunts, Jasmine could hear the chatter of the local kids who had come to watch the tourist take her ride on the donkey. She pitied it, sauntered back inside, fetched a knife, grabbed its neck and started sawing at the rope. Her father and uncle were trying to get her attention but all she focused on was the animal and its freedom. The stupid donkey didn't move so she smacked its hind hard. Its leg bolted out backwards towards her uncle's shoulder. The crack was loud as he bellowed and fell to the floor. 'What have you done?' her father said.

'You left me here, sick and trapped in a house full of stranger's force feeding me food and sneaking around speaking in tongues in the dark. I hate it here. I hate you all.' Her Tata came towards her with her arms wide open but the heat shot through her blood, through her arms and hands and shoved into her soft belly. The old lady kneeled down gasping at the floor. Jasmine was shocked at the force released from her hands, feeling sorry instantly. It was too late to retract. Ashamed at the monster within, she fled down the street overwhelmed by the exotic land that had turned on her so cruelly.

Jasmine pulled at her collar. It tightened around her throat. Sweat shimmered on her forehead. She looked around the bar and, realising no one had noticed her, breathed slower. With the next breath she downed her cocktail in one gulp. Josh came back with two more drinks. He clunked them down on the solid table and sat down opposite her. 'Is it for a lot of money?' he said.

'What?'

'Your inheritance. I'm guessing it has got to be significant?' A smile flickered on her face. 'Well then, it must be worth trying?'

'I know. I know. But I don't have to go tonight.' Jasmine stood up, finished the blue cocktail mix, flicked Josh a smile and walked over to the bar. She needed an injection of alcohol, so downed a shot. The aniseed flavour burned her throat and set her chest on fire. She welcomed it, the delirious escape to take her mind off Jericho. She ordered another. The drink flowed easily for her but the conversation hit a stalling point. She noticed Josh change as he sat opposite her. He became uptight. He looked at her like a stranger. Jasmine became more engrossed in others around her, stingingly mocking their conversations. She spun around to get another drink, sending the tray of glasses crashing to the floor. She stumbled down to the bathroom. Leaning on the sink she stared at her reflection in the mirror. Glazed eyes stared back at her, dark hair wrapped itself around her neck. A piece of smashed glass was gripped in her hand, revealing itself as she washed away the blood.

Back at the bar, Josh tried in vain to get her to leave. When the bar tender refused to serve her anymore, he took her outside, staggering onto the street. 'What's your problem?' Jasmine said.

'You have had too much to drink. You need to go back to your hotel, Jasmine.'

'What are you? My bodyguard?' Josh hailed down a taxi. He put Jasmine inside and propped her upright whilst strapping the seatbelt around her waist, closing the door behind her. He handed over the taxi fare, said something incomprehensible to the driver, looked at her one final time and walked away. The car started. 'Where are you taking me?' asked Jasmine suspiciously as the Old City walls disappeared. 'Stop the car! I don't trust any of you.' She started pulling at the door handle. 'You've locked me in! You better let me out now or I am calling the police.' Jasmine took out her phone and tried to dial 999. The taxi screeched to a halt. The driver jumped out and unlocked the door. 'Fine, get out here.' He muttered something else she knew to be disdain, then drove off.

She stumbled onto the quiet road, the street lanterns providing pools of orange light but not enough to remove the shadows between them. A car slowed down as it passed her staggering silhouette. A group of young lads bellowed from the sunroof and turned the car around to pass her again. One of the lads opened the car door and grabbed her wrist. 'Get off!' she screamed, and ran into an alleyway. She could hear the car racing off in the distance with immature laughter bellowing out into the air. A bone crunched beneath her foot. Her ankle twisted as she fell to the floor. Staring up at the sky, the stars spun and the moon dulled. As her eyes closed, she tilted her head towards the houses. Something watched her from a window.

***

Heavy grey clouds blocked out the sun and fell low in the cold, daytime air. She tried to run but the snow covered ground swallowed up her thin ankles, pulling her down. A thunderous bang rang out. It pierced her ears and pinned her body to the ground. She lay still. A warm stream trickled past her face. She looked up to see the snow stained a deep red. She stumbled forward, wiping the wetness from her face. A hyena slouched over the deer's twitching carcass, tearing its flesh as its blood drained into the snow.

CHAPTER 7

Jasmine's head throbbed as she tried to sit up. She didn't recognise the room. Its uneven stone floor was partly covered with worn woollen rugs. A reading lamp and a wooden desk sat against white walls and two tapestries with Arabic calligraphy, stitched with gold thread, hung on the wall opposite her. Visions of the previous night flashed back to her; Josh, the taxi, the lonely street. She swung her legs down and winced. A veiled figure ran towards her.

'Sit, sit,' said the woman, kneeling next to the bed. Her soft voice soothed her. Jasmine looked at her ankle, bound with bandages. 'Hiba,' she said, lifting her veil. 'You?'

'Jasmine.'

'Do you know that drink is the mother of evils?' said Hiba, 'You must be careful here. Especially you.'

'Why?'

'You are a Palestinian girl, no?'

'Does that matter? Are you?'

Hiba nodded and said, 'I brought you inside. You must be lost.'

'I am, yes,' she replied, unsure of whether it was a question or observation. 'I'm looking for someone.'

'Who?'

'My father, Ibrahim Nazheer. He used to live here. A long time ago.'

'Nazheer. Yes, I can see it.' Tears welled in Jasmine's eyes. She pressed her ankle to detract herself from the slicing pain in her heart. As if dredging up her abandonment wasn't enough, the voices were back in her head again.

The remaining glimmer of hope was dragged out of Jasmine when her mother's diagnosis became terminal. She had become a vessel filled with disappointment and resentment. Then, when the practicalities of her mother's imminent death became the norm, she started to focus on her inheritance. Outside the walls of her mother's sick bay, the money would buy her a new future. Her vision became clearer. The excitement crept in as her brain began to believe in it. She had had found her future amidst the darkness. The shame of her egocentric self now made her feel uncomfortable. Jasmine looked around at Hiba's basic house. *How can someone be happy with just this?*

'I don't belong here,' said Jasmine. She shook of the blanket Hiba had put back around her. 'Thank you for your help, but I have to go.'

'You do belong. You are from a family of survivors.'

'What do you mean?' She was intrigued enough to follow her into the main room. Hiba placed an old map of Palestine on the floor. 'Your Tata, she came from this village,' said Hiba pointing to a pencilled-in location. 'And your father, I believe he was last seen in Betein.' Her finger showed Jasmine a northern town not too far from Jerusalem ringed on the map.

'Tell me, how do you know about him and my Tata?'

'There aren't many of us left. We look after each other.' Soon after, Hiba made a breakfast of Arabic flat bread, herbs and sweet mint tea. They sat and ate together whilst the day warmed up outside the window. Jasmine showed Hiba her appreciation in the only way she knew how, but Hiba kept her hands pinned to her chest. 'For *Allah*,' said

Hiba.

Jasmine slipped the money onto a side table and walked outside onto the street. The neighbourhood was run down but it didn't bring with it the fear she had felt last night. She made it back to the main road and waved down a taxi. 'The King David hotel,' said Jasmine. She felt the old map between her fingers and stared at the hopeful pen markings. The anticipation and requirement for a guide gave her enough courage to call Josh.

Back at the hotel, she was ready and packed for the journey ahead. She didn't know how long the trip was going to take, so she packed enough for an over-night stay. As the hotel lobby clock struck 10am Josh appeared, as he had promised. Her nerves tickled under her skin and heightened her senses. Her steps didn't seem natural and her hair wouldn't fall in the right place. She hoped her cheeks would stay fair and wouldn't give her away. When he turned to see her, his eyes lit with the light of a thousand fires and she felt her cheeks burn. 'I'm sorry about last night, Josh. It is all a bit too much to deal with right now.' Embarrassed at her own truthfulness and her failing resistance to him, she quickly rushed outside leaving Josh to follow. Climbing into his Jeep, she noticed a new map spread over the passenger seat and marked with red pen. 'I think I know where it is,' said Josh.

Jasmine took a deep breath as they headed off. She thought of Hiba and then about her own life and how she had felt, even before her mother's illness. She had everything she could have wanted, but she still drank herself to sleep most nights. 'How are you feeling today?' said Josh breaking the silence.

'A bit delicate.'

'It isn't good for you, that is why I don't like it,' Josh said.

'I know. I'm going to cut it out.'

'Why now?'

'I don't like what I've become.' She spoke honestly

with Josh which was unusual for her. The truth slipped from her mouth as easily as her lips moved. It was the first time she hadn't been putting on a front. She thought of her friends back home. They had known what was happening, but no one had visited. Before her mother became ill, the house bustled with people and parties. She would spend the evenings drinking and enjoying their company. It was fun but as the years wore on every conversation became the same and the stories that she had heard numerous times ate away at pieces of her sanity. So, instead, she numbed them through the copious, wine-tinted smog, until the nights became so wild she didn't know who she was anymore. She looked at Josh and she liked who she was with him. A part of her was emerging that she hadn't known in such a long time.

She had once dreamed of a different future; it was simpler then. Her childhood however was short-lived. Through the years, she had become defensive and learned to disassociate herself from everything her father stood for. She aligned herself solely with her English mother and her English heritage. It left a half of her unaccounted for, half of her story completely unknown and lost in the world. Deep down she knew, unless she explored it, the incompleteness would always hover over her. She didn't know what the day ahead could bring but for once it seemed to blossom with opportunities. Her mind began to create stories. *'Maybe the town would reveal the clue to what had happened to her father?'* As the breeze whipped around the open top Jeep, a tickle of hope danced through her. She wanted to learn more about her father and his family. She had never before realised her resemblance to her Tata either. Perhaps it was that half of her genes, made with the Palestinian strength her father often spoken of proudly, which would fight through.

The Jeep pulled through the country and left civilisation behind. The air became easier to breathe and olive trees appeared along the roadside and on the stepped hills surrounding them. A local Bedouin man tended to his herd. He reminded her of the first trip to Palestine with her father. She had seen a Bedouin family setting up their home. It was close enough to the roadside that she could see their sun-bleached, material tents willowing in the slight breeze of the winter day. 'Are they camping here?' she had asked her father. He slowed down the car and pulled off onto the dirt track that ran alongside the road, took her hand and walked down the rocky incline into the pit of the valley.

Jasmine stared at the brass medallions stitched into the Bedouin women's face veil. The veil pinched in above her nose and framed her dark eyes. Jasmine's father spoke Arabic to her husband who was tending to a sturdy looking camel. They had two sons. Fahed must have been about fourteen. He was well built, with burnt butter coloured skin and dark, wavy hair that fell around his chin. His younger brother, Khalid, was paler and his hair was a mop on his head that repeatedly fell into his eyes. Jasmine was the same age as Khalid. She proved far too interesting to ignore so he came over to her. He poured her an imaginary coffee into tiny cups for their imaginary tea party. Khalid spoke to Jasmine in a flurry of excited Arabic. He wasn't at all put off that she couldn't understand, he was satisfied with her enthusiasm. Fahed had grown bored of his childish younger brother and went outside to join his father. Khalid disappeared through a beaded curtain and reappeared a few minutes later with one of his mother's headpieces. He put it on Jasmine's face, tying it around the back of her head, rather gently considering his young but weathered hands. It was hot and heavy underneath the mesh of material. He spun her around to face a cracked mirror that leant against a stack of coloured woollen blankets. She looked at her reflection, her eyes framed loosely by the heavy medallions, her dark hair secretly tucked away. Khalid's face beamed from behind her at his handy work. Jasmine's father appeared as

Khalid excitedly danced around her heels. His voice flowed in twirls about his tongue. He pointed at Jasmine and skipped around her father. 'He wants to know if you will come back here to see him?' said Jasmine's father smiling, 'He's taken quite a liking to you.'

Khalid had lost concentration and disappeared again. He returned as Jasmine's father was thanking his parents for their hospitality. Khalid handed Jasmine some spare coins of medallions tied together by a thin piece of leather. She smiled at his warm face and thanked him for the gift. He spoke again to her father but this time in more hushed tones, running off bashfully before she could say goodbye. 'Well, it looks like you have a suitor,' he said. She watched Khalid wave to them in the distance as they drove off. Now, ten years later, she strained her eyes to see if she recognised the Bedouin who sat on the rock by the roadside.

Jasmine could not have known Khalid's fate. As the years ticked by after her first visit, Khalid's family had been restricted in their movement around the country. New Israeli settlements were built around their trails and barbed wire fences cut through the once open landscape. They weren't as imposing as the dense concrete blocks that cut up the Holy City, but they proved efficient in preventing the Bedouin from roaming freely. They were herded to smaller patches of land. Modern rectangular two-storey houses built under the Occupation sprung up, specifically at certain locations of interest and vantage points.

Khalid had taken his family's herd of goats to their usual watering hole. It was difficult to climb the rocky embankment, despite his sturdy legs. When he reached the top, his throat was dry so he crouched down near a stream and pressed his face into the water, drinking gulps until his thirst was satisfied. In his haste he failed to see a carcass rolled to the side of the water. He kicked over the body of the lynx. Its glassy eyes stared vacantly above, still unclouded and only recently dead. Khalid knew then he had made a fatal mistake. His tongue now sensed the powdery, acid tang which was the same taste the lynx would have had, only hers would have been heightened. The lynx hadn't been warned of the shadows that climbed down unsteadily from the hilltops under the cloak of the night sky. Khalid had. He would listen to his brother's stories as they sat out in the wilderness under the backdrop of the huge, white moon. His brother told him the seeds would grow as normal when the sun rose the morning after the shadows had come. But they weren't healthy. Inside them the poison had flowed into the soil and the chemicals turned parts of the streams toxic. The body of the lynx was a sign Khalid had missed. He struggled back to his camp and ringed the goats into their makeshift pen before finding his mother, his face grey with the fate that was about to befall him.

'I'm sorry,' he cried. 'I didn't check the water first. I brought the goats back before they had time to drink much. Do not go to the stream,' he pleaded.

'Tell me what happened, Khalid?' his mother whispered urgently in his ear, stroking the back of his head.

'I drank lots of water and I didn't check like I was taught too since the strangers came and there, when I had finished, I saw the dead lynx.'

His mother held him breathing away his tale, slowly inhaling the salt in the air from his streaming tears and sweat that glistened on his arms. She held him, listening to the fast pounding of his scared heart and took comfort in the fact it was beating hard and his warm, little body was still hers to hold.

That night a fever crept through Khalid, heating his blood. Sweat dripped from his writhing body. His head spun and played out hallucinations that danced amongst the mountains. Hunched figures cackled in the distance, and the moon that had always been so constant and comforting died in front of his eyes. He didn't make it to the morning.

***

On their way, Jasmine and Josh passed a small village. Old pastel coloured houses were built up on steep, narrow roads that led high into the hills. A church with a wooden cross stood in the centre enclosed by a white wooden fence and a pretty garden.

'I didn't realise Christians live here?' Jasmine said.

'Yes, they do. There's no trouble between the people of different faiths in these villages. They've lived side by side for thousands of years.' Jasmine felt the chill of the weather as the Jeep climbed higher. Josh looked at the slight goose-bumps on her arm and handed her his green hooded jumper from his lap. 'Here, put this on Miss, it's not as warm up here. I thought you would be used to it coming from England. Or is that just the rain?'

'Both actually. But after a week of sun, I'm not used to it. Maybe I will have to stay.' Jasmine answered jokingly, but something inside tugged at her. She pulled his jumper over her head and breathed his scent into her lungs. 'Thanks,' she almost whispered.

'You're welcome,' he answered, attentively. Boulders blocked the road up ahead so they turned left at the hefty road block and weaved past thorny bushes and wandering sheep, until they arrived at the village of Betein. Most of the shop's shutters were down and it seemed deserted. Parking up, they climbed out of the Jeep and continued on foot. Quaint houses lined the streets which rose and fell with the hills. They reminded Jasmine of the homes in Jericho. They turned down a road leading them further into the village, where the older houses were replaced by modern duplexes with emerald green tufty gardens shaded by huge, leafy trees. In the centre of the village stood a cream mosque. Its square exterior was topped by a sizable, onion-shaped dome decorated with traditional lattice work intricately cut into geometrical patterns and shapes around its circumference. Either side of the dome stood two tall minarets that reached above the roofs of the houses. The call to prayer sounded, vibrating through its speakers and infusing the air with its peaceful tone, summoning people to the afternoon prayer.

After the call, movement stirred from inside the houses which had appeared empty before. Sandals flopped against the stone floors, water gushed inside the washrooms as the faithful readied themselves for prayer. An elderly man dressed in a traditional white robe, holding turquoise prayer beads between his fingers, ambled down the street but stopped dead when he noticed Jasmine and Josh. Jasmine was taken aback by his almost knowing stare, but she greeted him and he moved on. Two boys played behind him as he walked, grappling with a ball between their feet. Their laughter stayed in the air until it was replaced with another call from the mosque.

More doors opened and locals gathered onto the street, heading towards the mosque. Josh took Jasmine's hand and led her away from the villagers down a shaded side road. A wooden stile took them over a stone wall and with the sound of the prayer intermittently breaking up the birdsong, they walked further away from the village until they were surrounded by countryside. They rested in a meadow, under the leaves of hundred-year-old trees still bearing plump fruits.

'I don't think we will find anything here,' mused Jasmine, gazing across the rolling fields. Mountains in the distance broke up the horizon.

'How did you find out about the village?' said Josh.

'I met this woman Hiba back in Jerusalem, she told me of this place and I read my father's book, apparently he knew people here, he interviewed some too. I was hoping to speak to Maria, the baker.'

'I haven't seen a bakery anywhere. Maybe we should ask someone?' Jasmine left Josh as he rested with his back against the tree trunk. Her legs were as restless as she was. She weaved through the trees and collected cherries and apricots in a makeshift pouch she had made with her top. She dropped handfuls off by Josh as he snoozed under the tree. She pulled out the articles and photographs in her backpack and sat in the shade, her eyes straining to re-read them again. She studied the photograph, the one of the hyena, the backdrop, the familiarity of the place echoed a memory somewhere in the recess of her mind. She had tasted these cherries before too, she knew that. With the articles revealing nothing new, the red book became a bunch of names and stories as distant as her father. She pulled out the letters.

Dear Papa,
Winter, 1941
I am writing this letter from a hospital bed in Bratislava. They found me between the roadside and the woods, nearly dead but for the fur I wore keeping me alive. Schmidt is the name of the man who found me. He keeps calling me a survivor. He says there aren't many young men who can survive, especially during war. I feel like the war started a long time ago. Schmidt often comes to see me at the hospital. He sits and listens to how I survived alone for weeks back in Germany and how I mapped out the route to take me to the coast. He seems fascinated by it. He asked if I wanted to be part of a new group. Their plan is to teach us how to farm, to look after the land and the animals. I relish such an opportunity. He tells me stories of our new home. He says it is warm there, filled with trees and fertile lands. He has been there before, many times. I hope to find you all there in a safe home at last. I pray for it every night.
Yours, Bert.

Dear Papa,
Spring, 1941
Schmidt has us working hard. We wake up at dawn and till the soil, plant seeds and take lessons about agriculture, diseases and pests. There is so much more to farming than planting seeds that I

had never known before! We have been here for months now. Some of the other Khalutsim don't believe we will ever leave. We will wait and see. At least we are relatively safe as the war tears Europe apart around us. I want to be a farmer now. Wherever I end up, it will have land that I can grow life on.

Yours, Bert.

Dear Papa,

Summer, 1942

The day has arrived. We left for Vienna before dawn broke this morning. I am writing this to you on one of our long train stops. It is a clandestine trip, so we are using the rail tracks at odd hours when there will be no one to watch. Every now and then, when we have to stop, the train driver turns out the lights and all I can hear is the breath of hundreds of people, cramped into the cabin with me. I pray we see the other end.

Yours, Bert.

Jasmine's forehead creased in confusion. *Who was he? Had her father told her about him?* She knew he hadn't written it, it wasn't his handwriting nor was he old enough to have been there in the 1930's, he wasn't even born. 'Hey,' Josh murmured, opening his eyes to Jasmine. 'How long have I been out?'

'Just long enough for me to draw a moustache on your face in permanent marker,' she joked.

He rubbed his upper lip and pulled the corners of his lips down, 'Oh I think it suits me,' he said stroking the imaginary moustache.

'I picked you some cherries.'

'Thank you,' he said, taking a bunch. 'They look good.'

'These aren't going to fill me up though,' he said, patting his stomach, 'do you want to go and make some proper lunch?'

'Sounds good to me.' Jasmine packed away the letters, the encroaching danger of war time Germany fading back into history as they walked the trail back. A procession of mourners gathered in the road up ahead. They carried a shrouded body above the crowd. 'It looks like the whole village has turned out,' said Josh. 'Let's go and take a closer look.'

'Why would we want to do that?'

'If you want to find the baker, then she's either here, or someone must know where we can find her.'

She wrapped her neck scarf around her head and joined the rear of the procession as they headed into the village's mosque. Inside the domed hall, smelling of musk, the men gathered around the Imam as he recited verses from the Quran over the body. Jasmine stood apart from the crowd at the back of the mosque, joined by one other woman her mother's age. Her hair was covered in a navy and black spotted scarf, she wore a thin wedding band on her left hand and her eyes were red, her cheeks tear stained. Jasmine handed her a fresh napkin from her pocket as the opening verse of the Quran, *Al Fatihah*, was recited by the men in front. The next words Jasmine recognised were the prayers the men made to save him from the hell-fire. 'I'm sorry for your loss,' Jasmine said, despite the words sounding patronising as they came out. She tried again. 'Being alone is not a good feeling.'

'You are never alone,' the woman answered defiantly whilst pointing her finger skywards.

'Except when you die,' said Jasmine,

The woman looked sideways at Jasmine as though she hadn't understood. 'Especially not in death, Miss Nazheer,' she said raising her eyebrows.

Jasmine turned her eyes to the floor, regretful of her statement. *'You know well enough you are never alone,'* her father's voice whispered in her head. 'How do you know me?'

'You must be a Nazheer. You look like your grandmother.'

'Perhaps you can help me then, I'm looking for Maria, the baker. Do you know where she is?' The woman's face turned away. Jasmine couldn't tell if it was confusion or annoyance at being interrupted whilst she grieved. '*Assalam Alaikom*,' said in unison ended the service. Jasmine followed the men outside as the crowd moved and lost the grieving woman. The men lowered the body, on his right side with his head turned towards Mecca, and shovelled soil over him until the white shroud had been covered. Jasmine watched the mourners disperse onto the streets, hoping for another glimpse of the woman. A middle aged man remained next to her. She turned to him and he smiled. 'Do you know how he died?' Jasmine said.

'Shot.' He grunted and moved away from Jasmine. After a long suck on a cigarette, he came back. 'If he were to come alive again, he would choose this death as many times as *Allah* would allow. There is no better way to die than for Him.' In his eyes, she saw the same defiance she had seen in Hiba. She had seen it before in her father too. She remembered how different it had been at her mother's funeral.

The priest's words had echoed in the hall but Jasmine barely heard them. The mourners sat in pews in their Sunday best and wept beneath designer head pieces. The words uttered in the vacuous church provided no comfort. The funeral resembled a pomp ceremony; the choice of hymns, her face painted to look alive and the clothes selected for the burial. Jasmine wanted to scream and tell them all she didn't want to dress her mother for burial, it didn't matter what clothes she wore because she was gone. Her mother's face smiled into the crowd from a gold framed, larger than life photograph. '*Please be smiling now, mother.*' Jasmine had thought. The photograph was taken years earlier, in the time that had passed since then, she had become a ghost of her former self. She had lost so much weight that her skin sagged from her bones and her hair fell out until there was nothing left. Jasmine was shocked to see how beautiful she was like that. She wanted to honour her naturalness, but the funeral director gasped when Jasmine suggested a more recent photograph.

It wasn't just her physical appearance that changed. The doctors couldn't officially diagnose the mental disease that Jasmine knew manifested itself in her mind. She hadn't realised her mother's mental deterioration would have affected her inheritance. She thought her mother would have spoken to her about it first. The reasons for her being here drew her away from the past, her eyes focusing until she saw the woman being helped home with the aid of a man and a young girl.

'*Assalam Alaikom,*' said Jasmine, jogging towards them. 'I'm sorry to ask you at this difficult time, but please, I am looking for my father. He spoke with Maria, the baker...'

The young girl made a 'tut' sound with her tongue and spoke to her mother in Arabic. Her mother raised her hand as though she hadn't the energy to argue. 'Where are you staying, Miss Nazheer?'

'I haven't worked that out yet, but-'

'The summer house, it is empty, you should stay there. It belongs to your family,' said the woman, rubbing her forehead and wheezing.

'Do you know anything about my father?' The woman turned away. The man waved Jasmine along and pointed to an abandoned house set back from the road. Jasmine was so immersed in the funeral that she hadn't thought about Josh. He wasn't anywhere to be seen. A familiar feeling crept inside her as she approached the house. She pushed the gate. It creaked loudly as it opened then snapped back shut, trapping her inside.

CHAPTER 8

The snow was cold on her feet. She followed the trail that wound through it. The hyena had gone. The deer had transformed into that of a young boy. She tried to lift his body from the snow but she was powerless. He knew her name. He moaned softly for her to help him, his voice died and his sobbing was replaced with strained gasps followed by a deadly silence.

'Jasmine, it's me,' said Josh, opening the gate behind her and walking by her side to the front door, 'Here, let me.' He shielded her body with his as he tried the door of the single storey house. It opened stiffly. The window shutters were pinned back to the wall and mosquito nets were nailed into the frames filling the void. The floor was made of natural stone, as were the walls and flat-topped roof. Jasmine flicked a switch on the wall. A whirring, chopping sound started above her head. She darted straight into Josh's arms. He pointed up at the ceiling fan, his eyebrows raised.

'Sorry, I didn't mean to startle you,' she said, feeling her cheeks flush. He smiled, which broke his concentrating face into the one she liked looking at. 'Are you expecting anyone?' Jasmine queried, as he cautiously opened doors and scanned the rooms.

'I'm covering all angles.'

There were five rooms altogether. Behind the entrance was a sitting room with a brown faux-velvet sofa suite pushed against the walls and a rectangular coffee table in between them. The second room was the kitchen. Jasmine glanced around, it was sparsely equipped with a stove, a large gas canister beneath it, a sink, a fridge and a heavily pitted wooden table pushed up against the wall with four chairs tucked underneath it. A cabinet stood at the far end of the kitchen stacked full of crockery, pots and pans. In the other rooms, neat piles of seemingly clean mattresses and blankets stacked in the corners. Jasmine put her bag down in the kitchen and opened the fridge, a gentle hum came from the door. There was no light inside but the chill was working. 'All clear,' Josh's voice sounded from behind her, his tone more relaxed now.

'The fridge is working,' Jasmine said back, 'guess I could stop here for the night.'

'We both will. It isn't safe to leave you alone.' She felt safe, but she didn't feel the need to argue with him. 'I'm going to see if I can find us some supplies for the night,' said Josh. She didn't respond. Her eyes had wandered out of the window and onto the field of pale grass behind the house. 'Water, milk, you know, the essentials so you can have your tea,' he joked.

'Sorry, yes. That's probably a good idea.' He came and stood by her side and followed her gaze to the empty field. Apprehension at the familiarity of it kept her fixated on the view.

'Don't go wandering too far, Jasmine. I won't be long. Ok?' Jasmine nodded and followed him out onto the courtyard. Josh set off on foot to find the nearest store. He looked behind at her and smiled. When he was out of sight, Jasmine turned around to scope out the property. The roof of the house was completely flat and looked easy enough to climb upon. She stood on the garden wall to the right of the house. Plants and old bark jutted from the soil and reeked of strong earth. They formed to make a slight bank that gave her more leverage. She climbed onto it and pulled herself up onto the roof, feeling the roughness of the grout between her fingertips. She could see the field ahead of her, to the right another meadow and to the left the road they had driven in on. A brick tower stood to the back of the field. The zoom on the camera took her closer to its guarded walls. She climbed down from the roof and walked to the end of the garden. A narrow courtyard, shaded with tangled knotted twigs, led her right up to the concrete boundary wall. Its middle half had crumbled in the centre leaving a low gap to climb. She made her way through and started walking out into the field, the lengths of dried grass whipping at her ankles. The air smelt of sweet straw. Something triggered in the back of her memory, wormed its way inside her and slid down her spine. A voice shouted in the distance, followed by a loud ringing sound. She kneeled down behind the grass, struggling to breath. It became hot, so unbearably hot.

In front of her a young boy was running with a toy aeroplane flying above his head. 'Neeeeoooown, Neeeeoown. Come on, Jasmine.' His young voice carried in the wind around them. Jasmine smiled despite her legs barely making it over the snow as she ran to keep up. She stumbled and fell. She pushed her hands down until she felt the ground beneath her palms. A deafening 'BANG' scared the birds from the sky. Another one followed. Frozen to the spot, face down in the snow, the boy's voice had stopped calling. Jasmine didn't hear it again.

***

Jasmine opened her eyes, feeling faint. She made out Josh's silhouette. He ran past her, some metres away from where she lay to a figure standing in the distance. He was shouting but she couldn't make out what he was saying, the language unrecognisable. Her eyes closed as she drifted again. The next time Jasmine opened her eyes, Josh was next to her. He had lifted her up in his arms and taken her inside, now hanging over her and wafting the air with a newspaper.

'What happened?'

'You must have fainted,' said Josh, his face pale. Her mind tried to rationalise the episode to the change in climate. She wasn't used to the Middle Eastern heat; it did funny things to her, she thought. Yet she couldn't stop thinking of the nightmare that had permeated the daylight, it stayed with her still and preoccupied her entirely.

She spent the day trying to rid her mind of the mugginess clouding her thoughts. She found some old shears around the back of the house and hacked away at the overgrown bushes that clambered over a brick barbecue built into the courtyard wall. She cleaned the barbecue with soapy water and a wire brush until it was ready to use. Josh came out after preparing the food and marvelled at her hard work. It had done the trick though, Jasmine hadn't thought of anything other than scrubbing and clearing. She carried on preoccupying herself, preparing salad in the kitchen, washing and drying the pots until they were gleaming and, when there was nothing more to do, she was drawn outside to the smell of burning charcoal. 'What are you cooking?' she said, looking over his shoulder at the hand-made kebabs on the barbecue.

'Halloumi, pepper and mushroom kebabs, corn and my own aubergine and rice dish, but that one isn't on the barbecue,' said Josh.

'Where is your meat?'

'You told me you don't eat meat.'

'I don't.'

'Well, that is why there isn't any.' Jasmine smiled to herself and resisted the urge to hold him. She moved away and went and sat in the shade of the cherry tree at the bottom of the courtyard. She watched Josh in his own world, tending to the food. She would have watched him all afternoon, but when he turned to her and smiled a knowing smile as if all her secrets were exposed, she grabbed the pile of letters and started to read.

Dear Papa,
Summer 1942
We reached the safe house, a disused hotel in Vienna. Half of it had been burned down but a charitable organisation set up inside the other half and provided us with lunch and clean clothes. We hadn't washed or eaten properly in days. We were happy to be off the cramped carriage but horror stories also painted the walls of the hotel. Refugees had been captured and sent back to face the Nazi's only days before our arrival. Some had refused and were executed on the spot. The town has a stronghold of liberalists in the south, who secretly work against the army, but the plague of Germany is spreading quickly. I wonder where you are, papa. I wonder if you are still in Germany or if you have made your escape and could be ahead of me or following me on my journey. Sometimes I think I have seen you through a breath-tinted carriage window or waiting with other people in the shadows of the towns harbouring us.
The Mediterranean coastal town we need to get to sits beyond a small village that's nestled in between rolling hills, but I dare not to dream too far ahead at the moment. We plan to barter our way with whatever we have. So far, we have cigarettes, my furs and pieces of jewellery. I hope it will be enough.
Yours, Bert.

Dear Papa,
Autumn 1942
Thirteen bodies lie dead so close to the shore that their last breaths were of the salty sea air. I was one of ten fortunate souls who made it through. We waited in a private house for weeks until we had news confirming the ship was arriving that evening. A Fishmonger van provided us transport, the painted smiling face of a turquoise fish looking at us from the side of it as we climbed in, its innards stinking of rotten fish. It reminded me of the sea and how far

we had come. We waited by the beach for hours sitting and staring at the horizon, praying that the Captain would come for us and not lose his nerve.

After I had paced the beach a hundred times, a light appeared on the horizon. We hid behind a pile of boulders and took it in turns to look out into the cove and up above us onto the road. If someone saw, it would be too late. When it was my turn to look, no cars passed, no trucks. It seemed it was only us and the ghostly apparition of the ship.

It moored as closely as it could to shore. We waded in and swam when the water rose above our heads, and climbed the nets with the crew helping us on-board. Hundreds of people lay on the deck exhausted. I was surprised to see mothers and young children scattered amongst the groups of men who had made the long journey out of war-torn central Europe. In the grey light I saw blonde curls dangle from a young girl's head. She stood just as Liora did; her frame the same thin, delicate frame that could barely hold her up. I ran to her, calling her name. She turned round and looked at me with haunted eyes that could not belong to a child so young. Alas she was not Liora.

Later, waves of relief washed over me as I sat dangling my feet over the deck. But when I closed my eyes I saw myself at the widow's house once again. This time it was clearer. Schmidt had told us it was called traumatic stress; your mind blocks out events that are too traumatic so you remember them in different ways and sometimes forget they happened altogether. With a feeling of finally being safe on-board the vessel, it happened, it came back to me. I have to tell you, papa, so you know. You have a right to know.

I didn't just run papa, I stopped even as they kept firing rounds at me. I looked back, hidden in the trees away from the widow's house. Liora lay face down in red snow, her body crumpled from the force of the bullet and her curls covered in fatty fragments of red. Mother saw it too. How I wish it wasn't the last thing mother saw. One head shot and her piercing scream stopped dead. They will never be with us, papa. You are my only hope.

I hear people on the ship talking. There are helpers everywhere who try to reunite families. I imagine that will be a wonderful day when I find you.

A week has passed since we boarded. It is hard to think of wonderful days aboard this ship. It isn't how I imagined sailing to be when I used to read about it in your magazines. The days are baking hot and when the storms roll in we have to go below deck. It is so cramped underneath that I can't breathe. It turns even the most patient men into animals.

When the waters are calm, we lower ropes down and scoop up buckets of salt water and tip them over our heads. I sit there soaked and cool. For those few minutes, I have a tiny slice of peace. Then, the clothes dry to my body and stick to my skin, suffocating me under the unrelenting harshness of the exposed sun. The food rations diminished two days ago. There wasn't much to start with, but rot took over some of the stores and now, well there is barely anything left. The drinking water is guarded by two of the armed crew mates. We are allowed one cup a day.

When the night comes, those who are well enough sit out on deck and listen to the sea. Loud splashes disturb its rhythm. They are the sounds of those who haven't made it.

I dream of our home land. I imagine the rolling fields and the hard land under my feet. It is a land I can make my own and harvest to give me the fruits of my labour.

I must go now, papa. The lead in the barometer has dropped dangerously low. I have never seen it so low. I am not sure the ship will survive. I hear its bones moaning to me that it cannot last much longer.

Yours, Bert.

'They are ready,' said Josh. He walked over to Jasmine with a plate in his hand and a smile on his face.

'Thank you,' she said.

'What are you reading?'

'I'm not sure. They're letters I found in my father's things.'

'Do you think they will help you find him?'

'It doesn't seem like it at the moment but I haven't finished them yet.' They both sat down together, enjoying the shade and the food which tasted sweeter because it was hand crafted for her. When they had finished, Jasmine popped inside to make tea and clear the pots away. She was interrupted by a knock at the door. The neighbour from next door had come to introduce herself. 'Will you be staying long?' Haneen queried, after making her acquaintance.

'No, I don't think so,' Jasmine replied. 'Just a couple of days I think.'

'Why don't you join us for dinner this evening?'

'Thank you but I have just eaten,' said Jasmine.

'You can't survive on one meal a day and I will not take no for an answer. I know the old cooker there doesn't work. It hasn't worked in years. Eight. We will eat at eight after *Ishr* prayer.'

Jasmine agreed, she had a feeling Haneen wouldn't leave until she did. When she told Josh about the evening supper, he explained he had to disappear, he would return when she did.

That evening, beneath the cool blanket of the night sky, Jasmine could hear preparations next door. She closed the door and wrapped a shawl around her to keep warm against the mountain air. She was invited around the back of the house into a large established garden with a paved area well-worn from hosting. Haneen introduced her to her husband Omar, a thick-set man who stood proudly with his new wife on his arm. Haneen embraced Jasmine and welcomed her, speaking very good English with an American accent. Her friend, Mira, followed by her husband Mustafa, joined them too. Their daughter Malik lay soundly asleep in a Moses basket by the table in the courtyard.

'It is a lovely village,' Jasmine said, feeling a little out of place.

'And it is a lot cooler than most of the villages,' Haneen replied. 'Believe it or not we have snow in the winters here. Last year it was five inches thick.'

'Perfect deer hunting weather in the snow,' Omar joined in.

'Not that it makes you any better at it!' Haneen joked.

'Without a gun, it's more of a sport to enjoy the snow.'

'Without a gun?' Jasmine questioned.

'Only the settlers are allowed guns,' Omar replied, pointing to the settlements on the hilltops just outside the village. Jasmine remembered the checkpoints she had passed on the way through with Josh. Israeli housing settlements had been built amongst Palestinian land throughout the West Bank. They were easily distinguishable from the Arab's older more traditional houses. The colony houses were modern looking, set amongst well maintained roads, usually higher on a hilltop and always surrounded by barbed wire fencing, stone walls and army checkpoints to stop people wandering through. Identity papers were to be carried at all times to pass through the checkpoints.

Food was served and savoured. As the sweet mint tea was poured and the smoke blew from the bubbling shisha, stories floated into the air and became darker as night fell. Mustafa told Jasmine how Betein had changed in the last ten years, how streets and houses had fallen into disrepair whilst settlements and checkpoints broke up more land. During the night, army trucks rolled through at unusual times. Every so often a light glinted from the dead field behind their house.

Jasmine watched his thin, hunched frame bent into his wooden chair. His figure made him appear a decade older than his years. He had spent his youth trying to make a living as a carpenter. He would spend hours toiling in his workshop making one off pieces for newly married couples moving into their first home. Their first crib for their new-born baby, a few years later a bed for their growing child. But the customers came less and less as his country slowly shifted. The Occupation tightened its hold, businesses collapsed, export was prohibited. No one could afford his work anymore. He hesitated as he spoke more challengingly of their situation. His dark eyes glanced at his rounder, more assured wife who gave a firm approving nod which allowed him to continue. His voice strained as though he wasn't used to an audience but he was compelled to carry on. Jasmine leaned in closer to listen. His voice became quiet.

'During the night, when there's still hours before the sun rises, unusual sounds float from the hillside. On some nights you can catch glimpses of strange figures with frog-like eyes. They leave the turret in the field and head towards the hills. One by one they are swallowed up, disappearing as if they were never there in the first place. After the figures disappear, the ground shakes and the ripples die out just before sun rise,'

'What is happening there?' Jasmine whispered.

'I am not sure. But something secretive,' he answered. 'A special type of sage grows wild in the fields. We boil the water and stew tea with the freshly picked herbs, just like we always have. Yet now bitterness clings to your mouth. Perhaps that holds the secret to what is happening in the hillside?'

'Why don't you go closer to have a look?' Jasmine asked, trying to find some logic in the story. 'Go and find out.'

'If only it was that simple,' Omar interjected. 'Have you not noticed the huge boulders that block us from wandering freely in our own land?'

Jasmine nodded, not really knowing what this had to do with exploring the fields. 'I thought they were just road blocks?' answered Jasmine.

'They are whatever they want them to be. They appear overnight in new places. Roads, entrances to fields and farms. Sometimes people do climb over them. But there is no guarantee they will return.'

'People who have tried it have gone missing, Jasmine,' Haneen broke in quietly.

'Karim the baker's son, boasted to his school friends about sneaking past a boulder checkpoint at night. The next day he came home from school many hours late. It was unusual for him, but not unusual enough to cause concern. But then it happened more often. His father collared his friends in town demanding to know where he was, but they couldn't tell. Slowly, Karim changed. He alienated himself from his family and lurked closely to the walls of people's houses listening to their hushed conversations insides. His moods rose and fell with no apparent triggers or reason, worsening until the day he never returned home.'

'Talk circulated. Sometimes the soldiers use them as spies,' said Mustafa.

'Or sometimes people are misguided by the *Jinn*. They can shift and turn themselves into animals or people. They can infiltrate your dreams and tempt you to work with the enemy, tempt you into following a path you shouldn't,' said Haneen.

Jasmine sat there wondering about her own dreams. Her father's voice resonated from within her head as clear as if he was talking into her ear. *'You forgot about the Jinn, didn't you Jasmine? I warned you about them.'* His familiar voice took on a sinister edge this time, winding through her ear canal into her brain.

Her mind shot back to childhood. She remembered how haunted she had felt after a nightmare. Even in the bright, morning light her mind was somehow altered; a part of it clinging back to the shadows. She remembered the grey figure had stood motionless above her, looking over her as she awoke startled from sleep. She shouted for her father, expecting the figure to fade into the dream but it didn't. Her father opened her bedroom door. In the yellow light, she could still see its shadow. Her father whispered the Quran on Jasmine's head and only then did she see the figure fade. When morning arrived, her father spent it teaching Jasmine the words he had whispered to protect her. He explained to her how it may have been linked to the day she was born into the world in a fit of tears and blood. He had stood by her mother's bedside clutching her hand, terrified his new baby wouldn't survive. Jasmine's body had been lifeless as medics cluttered the room and surrounded her limp body. Doctors with stethoscopes and concentrating faces peered down onto the baby girl, perfectly formed but without life. They pumped oxygen into her blue lips as her mother and father looked on helplessly. A team surrounded the plastic cot she was placed on as red lights blinked urgently outside the doors. Organised panic took over as the resuscitation team was called in. Minutes passed that seemed to fill an eternity before God gave Jasmine her life. It could have happened in those few minutes after, her father said. He hadn't been able to get close enough to whisper the *athan* in her ears the moment she was born.

Haneen's voice interrupted her thoughts, 'The *Jinn* roam through the darkness here as hyenas, transformed in the cloak of night from their acceptable daytime facades. We caught one once. It snarled and spat and attacked the cage bars relentlessly with its sharp teeth, but by morning it had escaped.'

Jasmine remembered the photograph in her father's belongings. 'Are you afraid?' asked Jasmine.

'We do not fear anything in this world except for *Allah*. *Jinn* and humans are His creations and neither will escape justice. It is them that ought to be afraid,' answered Mustafa. His body straightened, bolder from the force of his belief. All four of them were joined in staunch agreement. It was a strength Jasmine had seen throughout her journey.

'That is why I am here,' said Jasmine, 'to find my father, he also went missing. I have looked in Jerusalem and the search led me here. The baker you speak of, my father spoke to her and I am seeking her now for some answers.'

'What's your father's name?'

'Ibrahim, Ibrahim Nazheer.'

'I don't know about your father, but I know you are a Nazheer, and I know of your family. There's an old story about them. Do you know it?'

'I don't think so.'

'Back when your grandmother was a bit younger than you now, she lived with her family in a village, similar to this one. It was on the eve of the *Nakba*,' Omar said. He looked at Haneen whose face had turned sombre. Hesitantly, he carried on, 'The army came through. They murdered everyone in the sight; men, women and children, everyone, even the animals. Your grandmother hid in a secret cellar under the barn, below the slaughtered animals. She stayed down there for three days until a Bedouin man happened to found her. She was too traumatised to speak at first. Eventually, she told of the man who had killed her family, of the cold, piercing green eyes that stared down at her through the floorboards in the barn, with her family's blood stained across his face. The Bedouin man took her to Jericho where she stayed for the rest of her life.'

Baby Malik broke the mood with a snort as she spluttered in her sleep. 'And as we speak about inevitable death, *Alhamdulillah* for there is life to give thanks for,' Omar said with a smile.

'Jasmine, I will show you where the bakery is. Maybe you can visit her tomorrow?' Haneen broke in.

'Yes, please,' Jasmine's voice said as a whisper. *Why had her father never told her the story of her grandmother?*' She realised it must be approaching midnight so she thanked them for their hospitality. Haneen walked her outside and down to the gate of the summer house, turned around and pointed down a winding road that curved to the left and slid off down the hill. The bakery was down that road. They parted with fond goodbyes as Jasmine went back through the gate. A shadow approaching her from the courtyard made her freeze.

'Sorry. I didn't mean to scare you-'
'How long have you been there?' she started.
'Not long,'
But she could tell by the cold of his hand that Josh had
been there a while.

CHAPTER 9 JOSH PART 2

Earlier that evening he had watched from his Jeep as she joined the neighbours for dinner. Satisfied for her safety he drove to the abandoned town, deserted for over fifty years. He had chosen this particular town because he would be able to see if anyone followed him. Josh's Jeep tackled the pot holes with ease as he bumped along whilst his eyes scanned the roads behind him and in front. The road hadn't been repaired since the locals had left. No one had been back, not even to loot. Josh looked through the smashed glass windows as he passed. He slowed down, his eyes strained to see if the stories were true. Had people started to come back? He looked past broken shelves and long expired food, the shop floors looked like the pavements outside, covered with sand that would have given away any sign of human life. There were only animal prints.

Square box houses with flat roofs had been over-run by tough weeds and fauna that seemed to strangle any life from them. They had weakened over the years and parts lay crumbled. Graffiti sprayed streets and bullet ridden buildings were testament to its brutal past. He shuddered as images played out in front of him of the conflict they'd fled from amongst this now ruined town. His foot pressed the gas pedal hard, the roar of the engine blocked out the sounds of his subconscious.

After a few minutes Josh pulled up to the meeting place and stopped. He closed his door, the sound shattering the silence that surrounded him. Standing silently, he listened for another vehicle or any sign of life. He doubted even Angels would come here. He skulked down a narrow jitty that led to what seemed a dead end. He made out the shadow of a large, recognisable figure propped up against the wall at the end. He took his hands out of his pockets and wiped them down the side of his trousers. 'Did you find out?' Josh said.

'Yes my friend, I did. But if anyone catches you, it doesn't come from me Ok?'

'Sure.'

'I've never seen you this nervous, you aren't messing around with the 'roaches are you? You know we are better than them don't you?'

Josh hunched up his shoulders tensely, his fists curled by his sides. 'Hand it over then.' His accomplice sighed and handed over a piece of folded up note paper. 'How did you find it?'

'We all have our sources. I know someone on the inside. He knows most of them.'

Josh nodded, satisfied with the answer. Although it was impossible, he thought he could hear the sound of the sea behind the wall. He wrapped up the meeting and left. He looked back to see if he was being followed, but nothing emerged from the alley. Josh climbed into his Jeep and drove for an hour before convincing himself he was alone. He pulled over at the side of the mountainous road. He had held the paper wrapped over his steering wheel since. Gripped in his hands, the moisture had smudged the ink. His eyes strained around the black letters as he formed them into a legible word. He quickly folded the letter in case someone happened to be peering over him. A few moments passed as he allowed the information to sink in. It wasn't the news he had expected. He had imagined this would be closure, confirmation that he didn't need to get involved but this only confirmed that he had one last mission to complete.

He climbed out, kicked the door of the Jeep and tapped at his head, forcefully willing a plan to form inside his skull. He imagined security fences and watch towers in the middle of the desert, an impenetrable wall between him and his objective. He knew that finding it in the first place, alone, would be an arduous task. He saw himself dragged out, his cover blown, his hands clamped with handcuffs and thrown into isolation. The thought was real enough to make him sweat.

He sat and deliberated with himself, arguing each case. His head ticked with a plan. He calculated the risks, the measures to counteract them and the future he would have if he just walked away. The future was the same as his existence now, one where he lived but against everything he believed in. He knew it was worth the risk, he would finish off the job. He had to keep focused on his aim if he had any chance of a worthwhile life beyond this.

Josh dreamed of a different path from what his past had tried to define. His memories of childhood were vague and filled with conflict. One poignant memory of his father was the night before the accident happened. He couldn't be sure now if it was the night before or another less specific day that his memory created into something significant. His father had driven to the Port City of Haifa. He always took him to see the ships at Haifa. That afternoon they sat elevated above the city on the slightly damp grass, looking out to Mount Carmel until the sky turned mauve and brought with it the smell of extinguished birthday candles. Apartments jumbled on top of each other with cars parked on every spare bit of the street. Lights shone on the roads and glowed from almost every window pane in the built up metropolis which tumbled down near to the coast. There, dark ships sat on the waters unloading wares resembling colourful Lego boxes. The cranes towered into the sky and the quay stretched out into the sea, littered with ships either side of it.

Josh couldn't see the beauty in the Port like his father did. 'Sometimes a beauty in a place belongs to its history,' his father had told him, when Josh admitted his thoughts. And so, he told him the story of the sailor, one of the few memories Josh had of him. His father never told him where the sailor came from but it never mattered. The sailor's ship had arrived at dawn where he disembarked onto a stretch of shingle-rocked beach. He left after completing his business and went back to the solitary life of a seaman. Years later, as he looked overboard at the remains of a wrecked vessel in the water he saw bodies alive in the water. He pulled them onto his boat and asked where they were headed too. They told him they had planned to head to the port at Haifa. Intrigued, the sailor changed course and took his new passengers to the place he had once sailed to before. This time the shingle beach was a thriving port. Ships full of thousands of people, speaking many languages, disembarked after arduous, often treacherous journeys. Life bustled around the ports and homes were built quickly. The sailor stayed on at the port, hearing countless stories of sorrow and hope as they stood propping up the bars into the early hours, the conversations only ceasing when the sun rolled up signalling a new day.

His father spoke often of stories about the sailor's life. He would tell him about how he had felt a part of the building of the port city, his own hands physically grafting to build it into what it had become, about finally belonging somewhere other than the vast merciless ocean where, at times, the tide took him at will, yet never to find a shore for him until this one. This one had become his home.

The sailor's stories stayed with him and every so often

he would be reminded of one. They seemed to come alive at different points in Josh's life in people he met or places he visited around the country. It helped his father to stay alive through his stories.

Josh's natural guardian after his parent's untimely death was his grandfather, because he was the single surviving member of his family. He hadn't wanted to take on a child at his age. The truth is, his grandfather had no idea how to care for him but he had enough emotion left to know the boy needed him. Or perhaps it was the most selfish reason of a man wanting to right his wrongs by trying again. So from that day his grandfather moved into their house. Josh didn't learn love and companionship through his grandfather, instead it was the community. It was close knit and it was formed from a variety of backgrounds, joined together by the single ghost of their ancestor.

Josh never knew of his own father's dislike for his grandfather. He had seen Josh's grandfather as a cantankerous man who didn't know how to show love, a stiff man unresponsive to any of his needs. When Josh's father, as a child, fell from a tree and broke his leg, he limped to his father, crying in agony. His father slapped it with the back of his hand and told him to grow up and be a man. The following days he had tried to put his foot down and walk, until the swelling became so bad his mother had rushed him to hospital just before the gangrene set in.

A rift grew between the two parents and eventually they divorced. So Josh's father, Benjamin, grew up with his mother. He saw his father years later when his mother died. Josh's grandfather sought to make amends with him soon after. Tragically, it seemed to come too late. Only six months later he would be burying Benjamin and his wife, leaving behind their beloved young son, Josh.

It wasn't a terrible thing for Josh to endure as his father might have thought, had he been alive. Josh was able to enjoy his grandfather in ways he never had. He would listen to his stories which were uncannily the same as what his father had told him. But he would still wake up crying in the middle of the night demanding to be comforted by his papa or his mama. His mind would construct them back into Josh's life each morning so his grandfather was left to remind him repeatedly of their absence and to ease the pain, he would try and console him by telling him about the Angels that stayed either side of him, so that even in the darkest nights he was never truly alone.

As the years passed by their house seemed to stay exactly as it was. The streets around them barely changed. The families in the houses grew older, their faces becoming weathered like the wood on the houses, expanding and contracting until their stories were etched into them. The houses stood like matching boxes up and down a model street with square patches of gardens, all the same size, separated by white picket suburban fences. Josh would avoid the streets that lay past them. He avoided the scuffles beyond the borders until it became his duty not to. Then he was forced into being part of the underbelly thriving in the streets.

He thought his grandfather would be proud of him when he came of age. He thought he would admit that Josh in some way reminded him of his old days when he was the same age, but he never said that and he never spoke of the old days. He told Josh about his childhood, snippets from his adulthood but nothing else. Josh used to tell his friends about his grandfather's old war stories as they swapped theirs, but Josh lied, his grandfather hadn't told him one. Instead, Josh made up tales full of bravado and heroic acts. Josh knew now, anyone with blood on their hands would know they were made up because there was no goodness in the taking of another soul. Instead, it left a black stain on the taker.

Josh wanted his own future and he believed he had just discovered a way of taking one for himself. His plan had to work. As he plotted, he immediately shook off the feeling of treachery that trickled into his veins, preferring to think instead that this path led to the opportunity for the life he had always dreamed of.

He read the note again and then pulled out a pack of matches from his glove compartment. He struck a match and set fire to the note, the fragments of ash disappearing into the mountain air. His clothes smelt slightly charred and the sweat patches under his arms had marked his T-shirt. He pulled out another T-shirt from the spare bag in the Jeep, changed and climbed in.

The thought of seeing Jasmine made his heart drop. He pressed his foot onto the gas pedal and prayed that the journey back would be long enough to erase the signs of betrayal from his face. There was no turning back now and there was one last stop on the route to make. The roads changed from unkempt to smoothly paved. The familiar house came into view as he pulled off the road onto the gravel drive. He unlocked the door to the house. It was dark inside but he knew the place so well it didn't matter. He weaved down the hall, trying not to disturb the sleeping man in the house. The basement was underneath the kitchen floor. It opened from a concealed trap door grooved into the floor. He walked down the stairs with his flashlight turned off. When he reached the bottom, he switched it on. As he did so, he turned and knocked the wall and in his haste dropped the flashlight on the floor. He held his breath. The house remained engulfed in silence. As Josh bent down to retrieve his light he noticed a draught coming from an uneven opening in the basement floor.

He pulled at the rotting wood to reveal a dust covered metal tin hidden underneath them. He looked around and glanced up towards the basement stairs. Still no sound. He opened the lid, the torchlight illuminating black and white photographs of dead bodies face down, slashed men and women in pools of blood. Children lay next to their lifeless bodies, some only noticeable because a chubby leg or arm was splayed out from underneath. An entire village lay dead. On the back of the photograph, coordinates were scrawled in black pen.

He took the photographs and buried the tin back, hastily covering it with the decomposed pieces of floor. He moved quickly to the corner of the basement, remembering to grab his passport from the safe and shined his flashlight back to the stairs. His eyes played tricks on him, a shadowy figure loomed over him from above the stairs. His breath stopped. He flashed the torch upwards in its direction but it revealed nothing. He climbed out from the basement and shut the trapdoor. The kitchen was empty. He ran outside, before jumping into his Jeep. He tried to start the engine, the key jammed and it wouldn't switch on. He twisted it again as its faithful noise emanated from the engine, and he sped off down the straight road. Just as he was about to fly around the bend he glanced back in his mirror, long enough to see an auburn glow appear from the downstairs windows.

When he was far enough away he allowed the wave of relief and anticipation to rush over his body. He had not known where the hope in his life would have come from a few weeks ago but the day he found her had saved him. He punched the steering wheel as he was reminded that it was in the most bitter of ways. He knew that they couldn't be together in this country as it was. His family's views were more segregated than the land. He had a different destiny, one that belonged to another world, a world a being like her could never be a part of. Logic had to overtake. He had been trained, he had learned logic, applied it to the most emotional of scenarios and it had always won. Although he felt himself weakening around her, he knew he couldn't give in to it. It was there as a test; a test of his strength.

He wouldn't have many more opportunities. Their time was slipping away from them. If he could leave, he could build a life somewhere new. He had never thought about it as strongly as he had done in that moment but the feeling of betrayal overwhelmed him. The stories of the sailor, his father had told him, were told to him for a reason. His father believed in him. His world used to be as clear as the sea his father told him of, like moving glass above the sea bed. But now it stirred up and drew out the silt and oil from underneath the dredges of the sand. He couldn't see past it.

For the first time in a long time he wished his father was there by his side so he could ask him what to do, but all that was left of him now were the memories of an imagined sailor and a broken dream.

CHAPTER 10

The sound of the *athan* sung into her ears. She opened her eyes and looked outside the square window, the sun hadn't yet risen. A gentle tapping sound on the inside door made her sit up. 'I'm awake,' she called. Josh was already dressed, his bag slung over his shoulders. 'Will I see you later then?' she said.

'That is the plan.' He opened the front door and closed it behind him, she listened to his footsteps fading, the gate creaking and the sound of his engine pull off. She threw off the covers, wrapped her shawl around her shoulders and went outside. The pre-dawn air smelt crisp and fresh, as if washed for the new day. She wandered to the gate and looked down the dark street. Men in white robes were walking in the direction of the mosque. Two veiled women jogged together, the white of their trainers flashing from under their *abayas* as they overtook the slower men kneading their prayers beads to keep count of their praises. *Those who find their way to the mosque in the dark, will have their paths lit to heaven,'* her father had once told her. Jasmine wrapped her hair up in her shawl and joined the faithful as they made their way to the congregational dawn prayer. She followed the exercising women in their *abayas* through the female prayer door. The coolness pressed into Jasmine's cheeks, the hall was lit with burnt ginger and purple diamond-cut lanterns suspended from the ceiling. Jasmine slipped off her plimsolls and slid them in next to the others in the shoe rack. Her feet sunk into the maroon and navy patterned carpet running up the stairs, twisting onto a landing with a washroom at one end and the prayer hall at the other.

Inside the washroom, she sat down on a marble bench the colour of midnight pine trees. Opposite the bench, brass taps protruded from the wall. A gleaming mirror was above them, decorated in tiny mosaics the colours of the lanterns that hung from the walls. Underneath the taps, between the bench, was a gated drain where Jasmine placed her bare feet. She rolled up her trousers and began to wash before the prayer. She rinsed her hands, her mouth, her nose and her face. She cupped running water, washing up to her elbows on both arms, over her hair, behind her ears and the back of her neck. Finally, she rinsed her feet up to her ankles. She looked at her reflection when she had finished with a slight smile on her face, she hadn't forgotten. She had done it with her father too many times to count but it had been years since, and yet it was automatic. She turned off the tap and dried herself with paper towels, wrapped her shawl around her hair and walked down the landing towards the female prayer hall. Under her breath she whispered in Arabic, *'In the name of Allah, oft forgiving, most merciful. I swear that you are the only God and your last prophet is Mohammed.'* The words wrapped around her tongue and fell effortlessly out of her mouth. She was joined by other veiled women and the two who had arrived before her. Jasmine stumbled slightly and looked around. *'Where do I sit? You don't walk behind people; no wait is it in front?'*

'Assalam Alaikom, sister.'

'Salam alaikom,' Jasmine replied, 'I mean, *wa alaikom assalam.'*

They smiled and called her to the front row, cream coloured lines ran parallel to each other across the floor, signifying where to stand. 'Come, pray next to us, *habibte*.' Jasmine's lips flicked into a faint, almost embarrassed smile. She placed her feet on the lines next to the two women, just as the second *athan* called. Jasmine couldn't remember the Arabic words for the prayer. Her foot tapped at the floor as she tried to recall them when her father's voice returned, *'Just be led by the Imam and put the intention to worship in your heart.'*

The prayer started and Jasmine mouthed the words spoken by the Imam as they echoed through the speakers and filtered through the windows from the minaret. They surrounded her, her body following suit to the ritual of the prayer. She bowed and placed her head on the mat, sat back on her knees and repeated it twice. They finished by saying, *'Assalam Alaikom'* to the Angels, who sat on their left and right sides, before the mosque fell quiet with the hushed praises and personal prayers of the worshippers to *Allah*, their hands cupped to the air.

Jasmine left the prayer hall. Her feet skipped down the carpeted stairs. She slipped on her plimsolls, still reciting as much Arabic as she could remember and walked out under the rising sun. A passer-by greeted her. 'Good morning,' said Jasmine.

'Sabbah al Noor.' Sunlight rolled over the hills and chased away the darkness. Young budding flowers spread their petals by the roadside, damp with dew. The fields turned to an expanse of rose gold and the sky was a cloudless blue. *'The light is good.'* She walked down the street, past the summer house and headed towards the bakery. The incline made her walk faster until she reached the bottom, panting and slightly out of breath. She felt rejuvenated and the scarlet flushed through to her cheeks.

While she caught her breath, she scanned the street for signs of the bakery. Amongst the good sized family houses and mature gardens that overran on to the street, she spotted a cove beneath a house where the unmistakeable smell of freshly baked bread wafted out. Jasmine peered through the entrance. 'BANG!' Two women were picking up brass pans from the floor. They looked up and seemed equally surprised to see her standing there. *'Assalam Alaikom,'* said Jasmine.

'Wa alaikom salam,' they said in unison as they continued to clean up after the spill.

'I am sorry to disturb you. I was hoping to find Maria?' Jasmine asked, looking around at the kneaded piles of dough on flat round baking trays and a blazing wood fire at the back of the bakery.

'Yes. I am Maria,' said the younger of two, as she patted the hard floor next to her.

'I wanted to ask you about my father, Ibrahim Nazheer.'

The elder lady stopped working. Maria paused. They both looked at each other in wonder.

'So you remember?' Jasmine questioned.

The elder lady started to beat the bread with her fists.

'Yes. But let's talk about it later,' Maria said. 'Come. See what we do here first.'

Jasmine ducked in and spent the rest of the morning being giggled at as they tried to teach her the traditional way of baking Arabic flatbread. Jasmine sat on the floor kneading the dough, then seasoned it and knitted herbs into it. She rolled it out with a heavy pin and placed it onto circular, smooth cooking boards which were placed into the wood fire. The delicious aromas of the bread baked with thyme and olive made her stomach rumble. Maria pulled out a blackened egg from the oven. She dipped it in water to cool it and cracked its shell before handing it to Jasmine with a baked misshapen piece of bread. Jasmine smiled as she took the piece of bread she had crafted earlier. Her teeth bit into the soft, dark egg and she sipped sweetened sage tea until she was quite satisfied.

After a flurry of morning customers, Maria led Jasmine

to her family's house just opposite the bakery. Her front garden was blanketed with grass and trees providing shade up to the front door of the house. Through a long hall, large square rooms turned off in different directions. The walls were decorated with handmade needle-work depicting homes and Quran verses in Arabic. Maria told her how she had sewn each one herself and was now teaching her daughter, Lulu, how to do the same. She led Jasmine into the sitting room and made tea as she talked about the original map of Palestine displayed on her wall which had taken her eight months to hand-stitch. The wire radio crackled into the room with news of the struggle happening in coastal Gaza. The reporter's voice spoke clearly enough through the haze, the room becoming alive with images of the recently bombed strip where hundreds of civilians, women and children, had perished from the Israeli onslaught as rockets rained down on them only days back. Jasmine's listening was interrupted by Lulu standing next to her in her pleated, navy school dress and heavy back pack by her feet.

'Hello, you must be Lulu. I'm Jasmine.'

'Hi Jasmine. How are you?' she said, articulating every letter as though she was practising her English.

'*Alhamdulillah*,' Jasmine replied as she helped clear away the drinks whilst Lulu spoke to her mother in Arabic.

'She wants you to meet Bambi,' said Maria, looking at Jasmine. Jasmine followed Lulu up a set of stairs at the top of the house and out onto the flat roof, decked out with an assortment of chairs, a table and scattered ragged ottomans. Stocky olive trees lined the horizon in rows, sat amongst stone wall strips winding around the hilltop. An Israeli settlement broke up the landscape. 'We love to sit here at night,' said Lulu, 'except for…'

'Except for what?' said Jasmine.

'When the olive trees go missing. They are older than my grandpa and his grandpa too!'

She skipped away with the flippancy of youth.

Jasmine's eyes focused on the hill, now seeing whole rows of uprooted trees dying in the sun while others stood trying to escape the scorching they had endured from human hands. Lulu took Jasmine's hand in hers and pulled her to a wire cage on the roof. 'Bambi, mamas here!' Lulu cooed into the sheltered compartment. Out of the shade a spindly-legged pale brown deer with burgundy spots on its hide slowly approached them. The deer looked at Jasmine with big bashful eyes as it nuzzled against Lulu.

'It's Bambi,' said Lulu excitedly.

'So I see! Where did you find her?'

'She was a baby when we found her out in the fields. Her mama had been killed and she was by her side crying.'

'Oh dear,' said Jasmine.

'She lives here with us now and she is very happy. We let her out into the gardens and the street because everyone knows Bambi.'

'Does she play in the fields?' Jasmine asked

'Not anymore. She's scared of the *Jinn* with the sharp teeth that killed her mummy.'

Maria stepped out onto the roof, 'Ok Lulu, I think it's time you left Jasmine alone,' she said sweetly, putting down a tray of drinks on the table. Jasmine pulled out the red book and saw Maria's eyes widen. 'So, you have his book?' she said.

'I have been reading it to find out what I can about what may have happened to him. He wrote about your son, Karim…' Jasmine stopped. Maria shifted uncomfortably in her chair, 'Sorry, I-'

'It's Ok. I just haven't spoken about him for so long.'

'If you don't want to, that's fine, I understand.'

'He was a good boy. He was,' Maria took a deep breath and sipped her juice. Her hands shook slightly as she pinched the tiny glass handle. 'It all happened so quickly. He became withdrawn, unhappy, and I pleaded with him to tell me what was happening. He said he could handle it. Then the weight started falling off and with it his time, as he disappeared in the evenings, until one day he never came back.' Maria took another sip of her drink, her lips quivered as some fell down her chin.

'Why did my father come to you?'

Maria looked down from the terrace to the streets below, then leaned in closer to Jasmine.

'Some of the villagers said that the army were targeting youngsters, getting them hooked on drugs, then bribing them with more if they provided information. He wanted to see if it was being reported, if it was happening.'

'Do you believe that it was?'

'I don't know. He wasn't going to the mosque and he had stopped his prayers. I think he got weak and the bad *Jinn* took hold of him.'

'What do you mean?'

'They can sense weakness when you pull away from our Lord. They whisper to you and you start to listen unguarded.' Jasmine shifted in her chair and lifted her eyes away from her. 'You know they are fearful of *Allah*'s words?' Maria continued, not waiting for an answer, 'That is what causes the *Jinn* to run away.'

'There are good *Jinn* too, no?'

'Yes, of course. There is always good.'

'And my father?'

'He was being noticed more and more for his interference and standing in the community. The army didn't like it.'

'Is that why he went missing?'

Maria put down her glass and looked straight through Jasmine. 'The summer house…you remember the summer house don't you, Jasmine?' she said.

'Yes that is where I am staying.'

Maria fell quiet for a few minutes. Jasmine could see her mind working furiously behind her eyes from the frown that fell over them. 'Try to come and see me again before you leave?' she said eventually.

'I will try,' replied Jasmine. 'Thank you for your help

today. You have been very kind to talk to me and tell me about your son.' Maria shrugged. Jasmine sensed it was time to go. Maria wasn't telling her everything but she had a right not to, it was her story. She said her goodbyes to Lulu and Maria and thanked them for showing her around their home. As she headed back to the summer house, she was happy to be caressed by the breeze that blew over her.

As she walked up the hill she noticed a large family gathering outside in their courtyard. Children played, women chatted to each other swapping hot dishes and scooping spoons of food into their mouths whilst men tended to meat sizzling on the barbecues. Memories flooded back of *Iftar* meals she used to cook with her father at Ramadan.

During the holy month of Ramadan, Jasmine's father would wake up before dawn and drive an hour to the nearest mosque. He would arrive back at the house a few hours after dawn to Jasmine waiting eagerly at the door. His smile always beamed at her as he scooped her up and then they would spend the day together with him reading passages of the Holy Quran out loud, stories of drowned pharaohs in Egypt, Jesus's travels through the holy cities and his fast in the secret caves of Jericho's Temptation Mountain. The tales would filter into their far removed English home and warm it up with a feverish excitement. About half an hour before sunset, they would walk out into the fields opposite the house, past the medieval church with the gargoyles, and up the grassy knoll. There was a gap in the trees just wide enough to see the sun sink below the horizon. The last glimmers of which would turn the grass into burnt gold, signalling the start of the evening when they would then make the journey back home to eat after the day's fast.

Jasmine would watch her father whisper his wishes and thanks to God, before ending his fast with a glass of iced water and the succulent flesh of sweet dates. Her mother would enter the dining room with her version of his favourite Palestinian dish; heaps of rice and roasted nuts hiding soft pieces of lamb and cauliflower. He would scoop spoons of yoghurt and helpings of pomegranate salad while they spent hours at the table, savouring the family feast.

At Eid when the fasting finished, her father chose the time after dinner to give her mother her present. Each year she was given an embellished bangle of twenty-four carat gold with engravings of Arabic calligraphy. Jasmine never knew what the inscriptions said, but she didn't need to as whatever it meant, it always brought tears to her mother's eyes.

When he left, the celebrations stopped. They had tried to host one together the following year but it resembled more of a memorial service. None of her mother's friends celebrated Eid and they often questioned why her mother continued in these celebrations, especially considering her husband had now left her. Christmas slowly started to replace Eid. Jasmine's house had never had a Christmas tree in it. Two years after he left, a knock at the door in early November, and Jasmine was greeted by a stranger struggling to deliver a large tree. 'I think you must have the wrong address?' Jasmine had said.

He huffed under the weight and struggled to pull out a piece of paper, 'Mrs Nazheer?'

Jasmine's mother had appeared, 'Ah yes it is beautiful! What are you doing Jasmine? Move out of the way, can't you see he's struggling?' Jasmine moved aside and let the man drag the Christmas tree into the lounge under her mother's instructions.

'But we never celebrated Christmas when father was here,' said Jasmine.

'He isn't here, is he?' snapped her mother. 'So it doesn't matter what your precious father thinks anymore does it?' Jasmine shut the door after the delivery man had left. She stood next to her mother as she marvelled at her tree. She explained it would look much better once it was decorated.

Of course, there were no decorations in the house. 'Do you want to come shopping with me and pick out some?' said her mother.

'Not really.'

'Fine. I will go by myself.' Jasmine heard the door slam and she went upstairs to her room. She pulled out some old things of her father's that she had collected since he went missing. A woollen sweater he used to wear and his pocket sized Quran embellished with gold detailing. She pressed her face into his jumper and smelt the burnt, golden grass. She cried into it until her mother returned home. As her mother tinkled about with the decorations for the tree, Jasmine pulled on the jumper and left the house. She walked out into the fields, ignored the gargoyles stare and sat on the hill until the field turned dark.

'Where have you been?' her mother said later when Jasmine returned. Her face grimaced when she saw Jasmine dressed in the tattered oversized jumper. 'I have been worried sick.' Jasmine turned to look at her just long enough to show her she had been crying. 'Come on, darling. Let me show you the tree. It looks even more beautiful now. It will cheer you up.'

Jasmine felt her mother's fingers glide over the surface of the jumper and wince. Her mother would have known it belonged to her father, so at that point Jasmine decided, instead of hurting her mother, she would feel some compassion in their shared grief. 'It is lovely,' said Jasmine, pressing a smile into her lips.

'See, we can have fun too, darling. This can be our little thing. I know it's different without him but we can't stay stuck in the past. We have to move on.'

After that Christmas it gradually became the norm for Jasmine. The Christmas tree came every year. It symbolised another year of her father's absence. Anger replaced nostalgia and the memories became polluted with the reality of abandonment. As Jasmine grew older, the

Christmas celebrations grew. She woke up in the morning to a champagne and salmon breakfast with her mother. The headache and fatigue had set in by the morning and the day loomed ahead of her. Bodies awash with sickly green and reds filled the rooms. The windows steamed up against the cold outside so Jasmine couldn't see out past the walls that hemmed in her house. The field of burnt gold turned into a vague a memory, as did the distant Middle Eastern sun, in the cold, English winter.

A woman walked over to her and spoke. Jasmine was lost in thought and hadn't noticed that she still stood outside the gate watching the family cook and laugh, like a child through the windows of a sweet shop. 'Come and join us,' said the woman.

Jasmine stuttered, embarrassed and flushed, 'Oh no. I can't sorry. I have to go.' She left swiftly. Back in the summer house, she showered and changed her clothes before curling up on the sofa.

The a*than* for the afternoon prayer called and woke her. There was still no sign of Josh and he hadn't called. She pottered around the kitchen, put away the pots on the draining board, shook the sleep from the blankets and folded them neatly in the corner. She looked around for something to do, opened her backpack and took out the letters.

Dear Papa,
Autumn, 1943
The ship we were aboard was battered into pieces by the merciless sea. I have never seen such forces before, monstrous black waves smashed down on us relentlessly. I couldn't see my hand in front of my face. I was one of the lucky few who scrambled into a lifeboat and abandoned the sinking ship just in time. Although it was a British naval ship cruising around Palestinian waters that had pulled me from the lifeboat, I know only God himself could have intervened to save me. I don't think I will ever leave the land I am on and venture into the sea again. It is not made for us. But my journey could have

ended much worse. Another ship anchored a few days after we were landed and those on board started a fire to protest, to come onto land, because the British don't want any more refugees arriving in Palestine. All I could do was watch balls of fire, hurling themselves into the ocean from my barred jail cell window. It burned out of control and I am told everyone on board died.

I have to be sure that God has some mercy. Perhaps I have had enough misfortune and I will be granted some hope to see you again, to find you here as more ships arrive. I will watch from the window. Hope will keep me alive.

Yours, Bert.

Jasmine's mind swam with packed ship decks and bodies burning in the daylight. She needed to cut the vision from her head. She went to the kitchen and boiled some water in a tin kettle. The teabag stewed for longer than she liked. Why had her father collected these letters? Nothing made sense. The four walls encroached her as dreams, stories and memories mixed together in a dizzying spell. Her digital clock flashed 17:06. Dusk would fall soon. She rushed outside onto the courtyard as she tried to regather herself. She didn't know her neighbour Haneen well but at least she had met them. *'I can go and buy something to take over? No, that would be too obvious. Maybe I could ask to borrow a lantern and they will invite me in?'* Her eyes strained and watched the sun as it threatened to disappear over the hills and leave her alone with the night. She walked over to the gate and unclipped the lock. She surged forward head down, if she didn't have the guts now she never would. She didn't reach the pavement. Her body bumped into a dark, strong figure disguised by the fall of night. She squealed. 'Jasmine it's me! Sorry, I didn't mean to scare you. Where are you going?' Josh's soft but firm voice sank into her ears. 'You look flustered, is everything Ok? Has something happened?' He looked over her the way he had done when she had fainted, his eyes deep with concern yet something more lay beyond them. He pressed his hands against her hot cheeks. His hands felt cold against them. Jasmine leaned into his palm.

'Can we just leave here for a bit? Maybe go for a drive?'

'Yes sure. Where would you like to go?'

'I don't know. Anywhere but here?'

'Ok,' said Josh. He opened the door of his Jeep and held out his arm. She climbed into the passenger side. The further they went, the better she started to feel. In silence, they drove down a steep winding road until the mountains fell into the background. Josh veered off road onto a track. The Jeep bounced over stones and matted sand. The land plateaued and ahead of them water as clear as glass flooded the land until it met mountains rising on the far side. 'I thought seeing as though you are a tourist, your trip wouldn't be complete without a dip in the Dead Sea.' Jasmine looked around. It didn't look like a beach and now seemed far removed from her first encounter with Josh. The edge of the water lapped weakly onto banks of dark, grey. 'There is no one here,' said Jasmine.

'Good, all the more for us,' he said as he stripped off his trousers and T-shirt and ran into the water. 'Come on in!' Jasmine sat in the passenger seat, her mouth wide open. Her eyes didn't leave him as paralysis took hold of her. She watched as Josh rolled over onto his front in the water. Jasmine saw his legs stick up at the back, then his hands at the front with his head high above the ripples he made. 'You have to have a go,' he called back to Jasmine.

She shook herself out of the trance, rolled up her trousers, took off her T-shirt until she was in just her spaghetti strapped top and waded into the surf. A chill rose through her legs and bit her stomach. There was no turning back now. She submerged her body beneath the water and was surprised at the warmth beneath the surface. The sinking bed beneath her feet made her feel unsteady. She didn't trust it to support her as she pushed her feet up awkwardly, forcing her body to slide forward. Her legs were free from the sea bed and her arms were stretched out in front of her. She tried to resist the urge to swim and stayed perfectly still. 'Well done. You have officially floated in the Dead Sea,' Josh shouted. She panicked and her face dipped into the water. The water, highly saline, overwhelmed her senses. She tried to find her footing on the sea bed, but flailed about splashing, unable to get her legs down from the surface. Josh swam over, reaching her in seconds and guided her towards the shore. 'Don't worry, it happens to a lot of first-timers.' He waded out of the water and pulled Jasmine on to the banks. His skin was pricked with the cold but he didn't seem to notice. Once they were out of the sea, he poured bottled water over their faces and rinsed away the salt. He sat down next to her and stared out over the moonlit sea. 'Nothing like a bit of near drowning experience to sort your head out, hey?' said Josh.

'Yes thanks. The fresh water helped. Now I know why people don't make it when they try to swim over to Jordan, even though it doesn't look far away.'

'Don't be fooled by it Jasmine, it is a lot further than you think. The sea can betray you in an instant.' The water rippled mildly in the darkness as if in agreement. She shivered as she thought of the seemingly peaceful lull trying to trick her towards a watery grave. 'We need to get you warm,' said Josh. He turned on the engine, switched the fans to heat and pulled out a towel and some spare trousers out of a bag. 'What are these?' asked Jasmine.

'You need to change. You are soaking wet.' Jasmine dressed behind the privacy of the Jeep door and looked down at her legs, swamped in Josh's trousers. 'I look ridiculous,' she said, as she presented herself to him around the front of the car in full view of the head lights. 'Nothing looks bad on you. You put me to shame.' He said winking at her. They climbed into the car, the heat warming their damp bodies. She rubbed her bare arms and draped Josh's jumper around her shoulders, pulling her knees up to her chest and resting her head on the window.

She tried to suppress a smile that snuck its way onto her lips.

The night sky glittered in constellations she hadn't seen before. The moon looked close enough to touch as it nestled above the mountains. She brought her eyes down from the sky and looked at Josh. His eyes looked tired beneath his thick lashes and brows. His bow lips crept into a smile. 'Do I have something on my face?' Josh asked.

Jasmine shook her head. *Just a lovely face.'* She recognised the Christian villages as they passed, the lights glowing through the small windows. The Jeep moved through the deserted streets in the small village of Betein, the brakes squeaking as they arrived at the summer house. Inside, Jasmine showered to rid the cracking layers of salt from her skin. She turned off the shower and dressed. 'Josh?' Jasmine walked out, still half wet. She lit a church candle and carried it into the darkness, illuminating the room enough for her to see it was empty. In the last room of the house, just off the kitchen, the light fell on a sleeping shadow in the corner of the room. Comforted that Josh was asleep she relaxed, allowing the night-time scene outside the window to remind her it was time to sleep.

A feeling of familiarity crept inside her again. She knew the field. The snow fell like jasmine flowers from the sky. They were in the field before the accident, before the snow turned red. A turret stood on the horizon. His laughter resonated through the air as he played. A glimmer caught her eye, the turret, death. A flash escaped from the nozzle, it screamed out and sliced through the air, entering and ripping through his small body. He screamed as he fell to the ground. She ran as fast as she could, hurtling herself downwards to his gasping frame. She couldn't feel the cold snow or hear the screams of panic that erupted in the distance behind them. All she could see was the face of the boy as he died before her eyes.

CHAPTER 11

Jasmine had to go outside around the back of the house. She had to go there with her dream still fresh in her head to put the reality of it to the test. With no idea what the time was, she opened the back door from her room and walked outside. She shuddered as an army truck rumbled past on the road. She walked the length of the garden to the broken boundary wall and stepped once again into the field. She looked at the turret in the left side of the field, it stood exactly where it had been in her nightmare. Her mind desperately searched to try and understand the relevance of her dreams. It wasn't just a nightmare.

The chambers in her brain opened, one after another as the reality dawned on her. They were memories playing out now she was back here. She started to see it differently, more clearly now. The field had been unrecognisable in the sweetness of spring, the grass long and shining under the sun. It was winter when she had visited with her father all those years ago. They had driven along the roads leaving Jericho, past the Bedouin, until they climbed into the colder climes of the remote mountain village. It was shortly after their visit when the nightmares had started; repressed because her young mind was unable to deal with the trauma of that day. So instead, it had locked them away in her subconscious.

But now the tragedy encompassed her as the realisation of events became clear. It was the boy, Ali who she had played with in the field behind the house. Bullets whipped through the air from the turret and sliced through his body. He was only eight when he was shot in the field by the soldier. They'd wandered over an invisible border they were too innocent to understand. The tragic murder replayed repeatedly in her mind until it was lucid. Jasmine saw him once again. She saw it all clearly now the haze of the nightmares had lifted. Ali died in her arms, his blood seeping into the snow.

Anger replaced fear and enraged her, she ran out further into the field, unaware of the eyes stalking her from the turret. 'You murderers!' Jasmine shouted, directing her screams towards it. It made sense now. That was the reason her father had returned, he wanted to fight for justice for Ali. The grass whipped at her legs once more trying to hold her back but she was older now, stronger. She surged forward until a hand clasped over her mouth and pulled her down into the grass, dragging her backwards her oppressor stumbled and lost grip. Lashing out with clenched fists she turned around and saw Josh, wide eyed staring back at her. 'What have you done?' he whispered in almost despair. 'Get back to the house. NOW!' Jasmine climbed over the wall and pushed open the back door. Josh followed, glancing behind as he went. Behind the walls of the house, he peered out the square, glassless window in the wall. 'What were you doing?'

'They murdered him Josh.'

'Who?'

'The soldiers. I came here with my father, when I was a child. I had blanked it out all these years. He was only eight years old.'

'I'm sorry Jasmine. I know how you feel.' He said, escaping her gaze and looking at the floor. 'Sometimes I forget what they look like.' She stared at him. 'You need to sleep though. It has been a long day,' said Josh looking back up at her. His hand pressed at his temples. 'We aren't going to change the world tonight.'

He wrapped a blanket around her shoulders and retired to the next room. But Jasmine didn't sleep. Shadows moved underneath the crack in the door, her worst fears danced in the darkness outside. It was the shadows her mother spoke of before her death. *The shadows are coming for me, Jasmine.*' She closed her eyes wishing it to be her imagination and not the madness approaching. Moments later, hands grabbed her and dragged her outside into the darkness of the night.

She struggled and writhed, trying to free herself from the powerful arms wrapped around her and her mouth. She lashed out and hit rubble. She was being taken over the wall behind the house and dragged into the field. Her body hit cold metal and something clicked. An engine revved loudly and pulled off with her in the back. It bumped along the uneven surface of the field. After a minute it stopped. Two doors slammed. Boots trudged off. Jasmine managed to pull the cover surrounding her and remove the muffle from her mouth. Her eyes strained to see. The men with the frog-like eyes, wearing army uniforms, disappeared into the hillside. She looked back desperately towards the direction of the house. She hoped to see Josh running through the field to rescue her but nothing stirred in the darkness.

Silence consumed her. Blood pumped through her veins, her hands relentlessly twisted and pulled at the ties around her wrists despite the bleeding. An inhuman yelp in the distance startled her. She stilled herself as her ears strained to hear past the silence. Footsteps padded through the field. The grass swayed and shadows moved within it. Whoever they were, they weren't coming from the hill. They were coming from the roadside. Silhouettes appeared walking differently to the soldiers who had captured her from the house, moving like the shadows. Their clothes were loose around their bodies and they wore *keffiyeh* scarves around their heads. She could make out the colourless pattern in the light of the moon. She tried to speak to them but her voice rasped in her throat and never made it past her lips. Hands took hold of her firmly and slid her out onto the ground. Damp fur brushed past her skin, the smell of a bleeding, wet dog assaulting her senses. It thudded into the truck like a chunk of meat. A swift movement cut through the air like a flapping wing. 'We are taking you, Jasmine.'

'Where?' she whispered. The figure didn't reply. Another engine started after a few chokes on the throttle, then they drove quickly, passing two villages. Jasmine could tell by the continuous artificial lights that broke up the patches of darkness. She braced herself as they pulled over. They took her out by the side of the road. Her eyes slowly adjusted. Four men with balaclavas stood next to a battered car as they looked around. Kneeling down on the floor next to her was an older man, saying her name. Jasmine looked at him incredulously, unable to form a response as his familiarity cut through her. It couldn't possibly be him.

'Father?'

'Jasmine, I am his brother Mohammed, your uncle.'

'How did you find me?'

'We have been keeping an eye on you since you arrived.' Jasmine looked puzzled, so he carried on. 'Everyone knows us here. Did you think you would arrive here and no one would inform us?' said Mohammed. He smiled. Then the question came. 'Why didn't you come to Jericho?'

'I didn't think you would want to see me…after what happened last time.'

He laughed softly. 'Jasmine, you were a child. You are my niece. You are always welcome in my home. Plus, the shoulders fixed as good as new,' he joked, swinging his arm out crookedly. 'As the father does so will the child.'

'What do you mean?'

'That is where your father was taken,' he said and pointed back to the direction of the field. 'And then I find you in the same position nearly ten years later.'

'What happened to him?'

'We do not know.'

A thud sounded from the boot of the car. 'What was that?' said Jasmine.

'Oh yes, we found someone else in the field following you. Perhaps you know him?'

A body was pulled out the boot of the car by two of the shrouded men. A scarf was unwrapped from his face. 'Josh! What did you do to him?' said Jasmine, her eyes scanning over him looking for injuries.

'He too was tracking the vehicle that took you. We didn't know whose side he was on so we took him to make sure,' said her uncle.

'And what would you have done with me?' said Josh.

'Probably thrown you into the sea,' Mohammed replied with a smirk.

Josh rolled his eyes and pushed forward, but Jasmine held his hand firmly. 'Wait. Please. If my father was taken by soldiers, then they will have a record of him somewhere?' she said, looking at her uncle.

'Perhaps. But there has been enough drama for one night and it still is not safe. They will soon be back and discover that you have been swapped for an animal, so we must get to safety and quickly. They will not stop once they realise they have been made fools of and the retribution may be harsh to other innocents, not just you. Come now.'

'Wait,' Josh pulled Jasmine close 'if you go, I can't protect you.'

'It's my family, Josh. We will go to Jericho. Meet me there?'

'Let him go, Jasmine,' said Mohammed loudly, whilst

ushering her into the car. Truck lights suddenly appeared from the east, in the direction of the summer house. The men shouted in Arabic and jumped into the car, the driver pulling off so quickly they hadn't even had time to close the doors. The car hurtled off the road. The engine over accelerated as it barely clung to the steep bank. With some force, it made it out and bounced along the uneven ground, trampling bushes and hitting rocks beneath its arches. Soon the houses and streets disappeared. The terrain became hard and uneven as they twisted into the wilderness. The car bumped and banged along for almost an hour. Her head started to thump and her body felt weak now the adrenaline was wearing off. She looked down the middle of the car and her eyes strained ahead to see past the windscreen. The ground churned beneath them. Dust blew in from the open window making it difficult for her to breathe and see. But the black lumps protruding from the earth grew and rose in to the silhouettes of mountains.

The driver shouted, '*Bism'Allah*,' whilst he pushed the gas pedal to the floor. Jasmine clung on to the seat, wide eyed at the uncertainty of what was to come. The car picked up speed and headed straight for the face of the mountain. 'Are you suicidal?' she screamed, trying to be heard amongst the madness. In those last moments before the car would unavoidably smash into the mountainside, Jasmine's world slowed down around her. She imagined her body thrown forward mercilessly at the face of the mountain. Crushed and broken. It was no longer the darkness that terrified her, it was her own mortality. Past memories of her life flashed by her eyes. They depicted a lost soul haunted by death. It had started with Ali, his small body scared and dying in the snow. She buried it so deeply she had forgotten it had ever happened yet it had sneaked through into her nightmares. The loss of her father, then her mother's fate which, although more natural, was just as soul destroying. 'Please God, give me one more chance,' she whispered.

The impact came. Her body was thrown forward so hard she lost her breath almost instantly, but it wasn't as forceful or as painful as she had imagined. She was suddenly overcome with the feeling that she was gliding. After a few seconds, she opened her eyes. From her slanted view outside the window she saw the earth on its side. The car was driving up the side of the mountain.

They almost free-fell down the other side, making her stomach rise into her mouth. But the feeling only heightened the sheer elation she felt at being alive. When the car hit a plateau at the bottom, they stopped. Her heart was pounding. 'We have to ride camels from here,' said her uncle. In the hidden cover between the rocky terrains, the camels waited patiently for their riders to return. From their saddles, Mohammed pulled out a thick, cotton scarf and wrapped it around Jasmine's face and hair. He pulled the rope, the camel obediently dropped to its knees. Jasmine stroked its tough fur and regretted it instantly as a repugnant smell of hay and manure was released up into the air. She swung herself reluctantly into its saddle. The camel stood up, hind legs first, tipping her forward before it straightened out. A cool breeze stirred and the sands whistled past her ears. The tyre tracks would be covered quickly. She relaxed in the gentle pace of the camel's gait as the small troupe trudged seemingly lost into the wilderness.

When they stopped, the men performed ablution with the earth. They made a row together, used the stars to pinpoint the direction and turned towards Mecca in Saudi Arabia, offering their night time prayers and, when they had finished, set up camp for the night that remained. Poles were stuck in the ground and draped in heavy goat's hair fabric which sheltered them from the wind. They unrolled bundles of blankets and started a fire in a pit of hollowed out ground filled with dried out twigs. Dates, nuts and Arabic bread were unravelled from skin bags. The Arabic bread was toasted above the fire and sprinkled with herbs and fat lumps of goat's cheese. Water was boiled in a copper kettle sat in the fire. Wild sage and tea was added to it and left to brew.

'Eat, Jasmine,' said her uncle.

'No I can't.'

'It's normal to be scared after what happened.'

'No it isn't that uncle.'

'Then what is it?' She felt the swell of tears filling up her throat as she tried to hold them back. Her voice choked underneath the pressure. 'It isn't fair that I am alive when Ali died. He was a child. I forgot about him for all those years and when I allowed myself to remember it was so much worse.'

'Why?'

'Because he deserved to live more than I did. He was always so sweet and loyal. No one had to answer for it. I realise now why my father came back, for justice for Ali. But I guess it didn't happen like it was supposed to.' She paused. 'I have money now uncle, well I will do soon. I can do something, pay someone, I know-'

'Money cannot fix everything,' he interrupted.

'But what about justice?'

'You think they will avoid it?' Jasmine shrugged. 'It is inevitable, whether they believe it or not, if not in this life then in the next. The Quran states, *"So whoever does an atom's weight of good will see it, and whoever does an atom's weight of evil will see it."*'

The tears subsided. The release had soothed her insides and provided some respite. It was replaced with fatigue. She watched as the men left the camp. 'Where are they going?' asked Jasmine.

'To a meeting.'

'Who are they are?'

'They are Bedouin fighters. They live to fight for our land, in *Allah*'s name.' He paused, before changing the subject, 'Tomorrow we will travel to Jericho, *Insha'Allah*. You will stay there until it is safe for you to go. Now it is time for you to get some sleep while it is still dark.'

'Ok, uncle. And thanks. Thanks for coming to rescue me.'

'*Bism'Allah*. It is my duty,' he said, retiring to the corner of the tent, 'and Jasmine, do not leave the tent.'

'Why, uncle?'

'Because of the hyenas.'

Jasmine had been afraid of them ever since her nightmares. She hadn't been sure if they were a figment of the local's imaginations or something darker like the *Jinn* shapeshifting between the day and night. Her eyelids were heavy and closed to images of hyenas and Josh, flipping back and forth. Then, the air carried with it the words she had heard from her father all those years ago. Her uncle's tongue curled around the letters and sounded them from deep within his throat. With them floating in the air, the images stopped and she drifted off to sleep.

She awoke what seemed like moments later to the sound of movement outside. She glanced at her uncle fast asleep in the corner. The fire had burned out, leaving silence and snuffed flames. She stepped outside. In the distance a hunched figure gnawed at something indiscernible on the ground. She crept closer and gasped.

It was a *Jinn* out there in the darkness, it had shifted into the shape of a hyena. The *Jinn* had haunted her back in England through her mother's tumultuous last nights and through her weaknesses here. She didn't know much about them, just broken memories of what her father told her and the stories of the families in Betein. She knew they inhabited the earth before humans, but they had created bloodshed between them and so God banished them to an island on the sea. They now lived amongst us. They couldn't be seen in their normal shapes which is why people were so wary of certain creatures. The misguided ones took on ugly forms. Jasmine imagined black dogs, snakes and of course, the hyena.

Now she stood alone with her nightmare. Its body

heaved while it tore flesh from the carcass on the floor. Its breath puffed out unevenly through its nostrils and disturbed the sand. The smell of flesh on its fur, lingered in the air and carried in the wind towards where she crouched. *'The Jinn can't harm me.'* They were almost a figment of her imagination, weren't they? She stood up from behind the boulder. The dark silhouettes of the mountains wrapped around them in a semi-circle and closed her in. She walked forward to get a closer look, now unafraid. She kicked stones beneath her feet, the sound breaking the silence. The hyena stopped eating. Jasmine didn't move but it had already seen her. It growled menacingly and walked towards her, confused and startled by another creature stalking it in the dark, a competitor for its carrion feast. Jasmine grabbed a rock from the ground. The hyena was close enough for Jasmine to taste its breath and now in range it leapt at her, its fangs bared in absolute rage ready to kill her without hesitation. She smashed the rock down onto its skull with all her force. The hyena fell at her feet with the force of the crack. Its scrawny frame writhed in pain and its helpless legs pawed at the ground. In the light of the stars, she saw its eyes weep. A flash of silver ended its pain as one of the men darted in and slit its throat.

'Are you hungry?' he said, with a grin, wiping the blood from his blade.

'I thought it was the *Jinn* following me here.' His face turned and became serious. He spoke in Arabic, his hands cupped towards the heavens. Jasmine went and washed off the hyena's blood from her hands. She was stunned that the creature of her nightmares was so weak, a desperate animal trying to survive. The sun edged up behind the mountains turning the sky navy as dawn began to break. She had had no sleep at all. The reminder that her time was running out only exhausted her further.

CHAPTER 12

They left and headed towards the city of Jericho, the oldest and lowest city in the world, the road spiralling down into the basin below the mountains. They drove further along the worn roads, where date trees stood alongside bright, coral coloured flowering bougainvillea trees, drooping their weary necks in the heat. Goats gnawed on grass in the fenced plots scattered around them. They arrived at the city square in the heart of Jericho, with jumbles of shops surrounding a courtyard in its centre. There, men dealt cards on wooden benches under the shade of trees while children played on the patchy grass. Plastic goods dangled from parasols outside the shops as the aroma of falafel and home-made bread wafted out onto the street from old bakeries.

Mohammed turned into a side street of houses much the same as those Jasmine had seen throughout her trip. Outside the houses, gardens ran onto one another without borders. They arrived at Mohammed's family's home, which had belonged to Jasmine's Tata before she died. Her aunty, Miriam was waiting for them on the courtyard. Mohammed was the eldest of three brothers and a younger sister. She knew the only surviving siblings of her father were Uncle Mohammed and his younger sister, Khadija. Miriam greeted them warmly and swiftly pulled out three chairs. Jasmine stared at the grounds, her rich memories faded into the dilapidated present. She couldn't believe it was the same place she had visited as a child. The wooden trellises with juicy grapes had long since vanished and out to the back, the orchard of lemon and orange trees she had once loved had gone. In its place, rubbish littered the desolate grounds. Poverty had taken hold. A tatty armchair sat under the shade of the sparse trees, against the backdrop of rugged mountains barely visible in the hot haze of the day. She sat down and joined her uncle. 'I want to find someone to talk to that can help us. There are many names that my father had, here in this book.'

'Here, let me see,' he said, gesturing to the record book Jasmine had pulled out onto her knee. He scanned the names and nodded his head. 'There is a wedding tonight. Most of the villagers will be there although many passed since then. Wait. These two,' he pointed out two names in the book, 'Musa and Saeed.'

'Do you think I could visit them?'

He paused and stroked his beard. '*Insha'Allah*, I can ask Saeed to speak to you tonight, but I'm not sure he will be much help-'

'If I can just speak to him myself, there might be something, anything.'

'Very well, but Musa, he is too old, he will not be going. *Insha'Allah*, we will visit him tomorrow.'

'Thank you, uncle. Thank you.' They sat and spoke of the troubles affecting the lands as she helped him to cut the vegetables that aunty Miriam brought to the table. Within the hour Miriam had been to the kitchen four times, each time returning with something different for their guest, freshly pressed fruit juice in glasses the colour of the sun, Arabic coffee steaming from the fragile tiny cups accompanied with a selection of sliced fruit, dates, nuts and cake.

Jasmine escaped the attention of food and went out into the gardens. The unkempt patchy grass hid stumps of what used to be the old orchard. Mohammed had explained that it was sometimes necessary to sacrifice things in order to survive. When she saw the billowing tents and the fresh, tiny cucumbers inside, flowering and swelling with five or more to a stem, she understood. Jericho's springs were drying up and the cucumber and tomatoes still sold well at the markets. The orchard had been sacrificed for their bread and butter.

Inside the cucumber tent, the humidity thumped Jasmine's body. A memory of her father hung inside there. He had proudly shown her around the farm where vines of tomatoes and chillies towered above her short height. *The best vegetables God grows, grow here. Jericho's pure spring water soaks through their roots and makes them what they are.*

On her return, Aunty Miriam showed her around their basic yet immaculate family house, four rooms and a larder all on one level. Miriam had dressed a bed with fresh linens in the only room with an air-conditioning unit. She pottered in a few moments later with a parcel wrapped in sheets of cream sugar paper. 'It is for you to wear to the wedding tonight.' Jasmine opened it and pulled out a hand embroidered dress. 'This is beautiful, you made this?' she said.

'I made it some years ago, it is a traditional Palestinian dress. My mother taught me how to sew.' Beneath her gentle exterior, Jasmine saw Miriam beam with pride. 'It was made to be worn, not wrapped in paper and left in my wardrobe. I think only someone as beautiful as you can wear such a dress. I never made it for me.' Miriam left and closed the door to allow Jasmine to sleep the afternoon away.

She awoke to the scent of blooming flowers filtering in through the open windows. She readied herself for the wedding. The dress felt like cool silk against her skin and the raised stitch work spun tales in gold, silver and turquoise over the black material, flattering every part of her. They drove behind the wedding procession beginning at the bride's family's house a few streets down. It seemed the whole of Jericho was invited, cars appeared from every side street with open windows, loud passengers and traditional music blaring from radios. The party gathered in a hall on the top floor of a concrete building riddled with bullet holes from its recent past. Inside the hall, tables covered in white pressed cloths were decorated with flowering roses, gold candles and confetti. Family approached Jasmine with greetings, kisses and introductions. They offered delayed condolences on the passing of her mother and blessed her father's name. She grimaced slightly at the reminder of her misfortune. 'Visit us again. Don't forget about us here.' They repeated enough to make guilt run through her veins.

Everyone returned to their seats as the bride and groomed danced down the neon lit aisle, the lights flashing to thumping disco music reverberating from the speakers. Miriam leaned over and told Jasmine that Saeed was waiting for her, so she slipped out of the side door. There was no-where else to go except for up a wooden ramp, a small sign pinned to the side of it read *Telephrique'*. She reached a row of cable cars. A young man, dressed casually in a polo shirt emerged from the ticketing booth and pointed towards the mountain, 'You go to Temptation Mount?' he said. She nodded, convinced Saeed would be at the end of wherever this went, and handed over twenty *Sheikl.* He closed the door, went back into the booth and pressed the controls. The cable car jolted outwards as it took her higher away from the ground. She focused her gaze on the twinkling lights which came from the mountain, that at a distance she had mistaken for stars. The cable car climbed closer until Jasmine could see that it wasn't just a round trip. Lights swung on the inside of open terraces on the mountain. The cable car stopped just inside the mountain ledge where two terraces either side had been formed. Shisha smoke and the smell of fried food drifted over to her as the hum of Arabic music floated in the cool air.

'Lemon juice, please,' she said as she approached the juice bar.

'Welcome. Is this your first time up here?' the barman said.

'Do I look that much like a tourist?' she laughed, stroking the traditional dress she was wearing. 'But, yes, it is. What is this place?'

'Temptation Mountain. It is where the Prophet Jesus was tempted by the Devil while spending forty days and forty nights in solitude in the mountain,' he said, gesturing to the other side. A staircase of steps led higher still to a stone entrance. She had almost forgotten the reason she had come. She glanced around, a handful of customers sat in the café all entrenched in their own conversations while the cable cars glided through the air back to where they had come from. She left her seat at the bar and walked up the first row of steps carved from the mountain that spiralled upwards. She wondered whose footsteps she was following, steeped in the history of the last thousands of years. An unusual feeling of being part of that history heightened her curiosity. As she approached the second staircase, a hunched man with a toothless smile straightened himself up and pulled out a table which opened to form a stand full of beaded necklaces and bracelets. 'Buy necklace, bracelet? I give good price,' he heckled.

'No, thank you,' Jasmine said back.

'This one, take this one it will protect you,' he said, handing her a bracelet with eyes staring up at her from each of its blue beads.

'No,' said Jasmine again, trying to hold back her annoyance. As quickly as she glanced away, the man had already clipped it around her wrist. 'No pay. No pay. Just take it. You need it,' he said. Before Jasmine had a chance to protest, he had packed away his table and hobbled swiftly down the steps. She shook her head in amazement and climbed higher until the only place left to go was through an arch-shaped door in the side of the mountain.

A sign hung outside saying, *'Closed to the public'*. The door stood ajar so she ignored the sign and walked into the caves, through the narrow pathways that led from one end to the other. Along the path, rooms with wooden doors emblazoned with a gold cross just below their frames had stained glass windows to screen the contents inside. Her hand touched the outside of the walls, feeling the rough rock beneath her fingers. Unusual coves filled with pictures and shadows were excavated into the rock, almost concealed entirely except for the wisps of cold air wrapping itself around her ankles. She peered inside them but only depictions stared back. She was now at the last door.

A *'No photos allowed'* sign was nailed onto it. Inside, paintings of religious figures hung on exposed walls, candlesticks flickered around the edges, glimmering in the corners of the narrow, rectangular room. Six steps had been built at the end of the room and at the top of them, as if to relay some significance in elevation, an imprint in a rock leant against the wall. Opposite it, a door led outside to a thin cantilevered balcony stretched along the monastery's face. Jasmine's eyes peered over the rail, at the bottom of the sheer drop lights glowed. She backed up against the outside wall as vertigo took over rational thoughts and images of falling flashed into her head. A faint sound she could only describe as cackling resonated around the mountains. Her attention was brought back inside by a figure breathing heavily in the space behind her. She turned around to find a bruised and bloody man on the floor, as the eyes of the saints stared down at him. She rushed over. 'Saeed?'

'There are eyes everywhere. You don't know who they

spy for...' he said, spitting out a fragment of broken tooth.

'Who did this to you?'

'They knew I was coming. We have to be quick.'

'We need to get you out of here. You need to go to a hospital...'

'No, Miss Nazheer, I fear there is not enough time for that, or for you. I came here to speak with you. I don't know where he is. Only *Allah* knows. I told your father he was getting too involved, that they had noticed him interfering, but he didn't stop. Not even for you. He wanted justice, someone had to be responsible for what was happening, he said. Have you read the stories?'

'Some of them, well most of them now, yes. Why?'

'Then you must not stay, digging up old secrets. Go and live your life away from here, let *Allah* be the one to take care of justice.'

'But I have to find him. Someone must be able to help me.'

'I need to tell you a story about where we are now,' said Saeed. He looked around the walls. 'You know the story about Jesus?' Jasmine nodded, so he continued. 'What you should know is the story of the gecko. This gecko slinked across this mountain and fell through a gap into the caves. The creature saw the figure of a man in the corner, praying to the heavens. It left and as it crept around Jericho searching for food it heard the stories of a fasting holy man murmur up to the drainpipes to where it was and, realising what a precious discovery it had stumbled upon, the gecko crawled back to the mountain and revealed where Jesus was to the Devil himself.'

'I don't understand.'

'You don't understand because you don't understand the country. Your father, before he...went, he told me to bring you here if you ever came back. He told me to show you our secrets so you would have a way out.'

'I don't want a way out. I want to find my father.' A bang startled them both. Saeed struggled to his feet, looking increasingly nervous. 'We have to leave. You have to leave.' He dragged himself over to the corner of the room. 'Look, Jasmine. Look here. If you need an escape this is where you come, exactly this point. Now go.'

'What about you, I can't leave-'

'Run, Jasmine!' The shout crushed him. He began coughing, blood spat out from his throat and scared Jasmine enough to move. She ran outside and fled down the stone steps. 'Help me,' she shouted. A waiter attending the customers jogged towards her. She grabbed his arm. 'You have to come, someone needs help. He is badly hurt, upstairs in the monastery.' He ran after her. Jasmine kicked open the door and didn't stop until she entered the room where she had left him. 'Saeed?' she gasped, 'Where are you?' She darted up the stairs, peered out onto the ledge. It was empty. The room was empty. 'Where is he?' the waiter asked, now looking annoyed.

'He was here, just a minute a go, I left him. He was in really bad shape.' The waiter slowly walked around peering into the shadowy spaces as if expecting a ghost. Jasmine stood in the empty room, her eyes searching for an answer. Underneath her feet, dried stains of deep red were the only sign he had been there. 'Wait, look at these,' she said, but the waiter had already gone. She retraced her steps and then left, barely concentrating as she stumbled down the stone steps. No cable cars were free to take her back so she wandered to the gift shop opposite them. The glass curved round the window and displayed an array of gifts. Jasmine went inside the cave where an elderly lady stood behind the till. 'Hello,' she chirped as Jasmine walked in. 'Anything in particular you are looking for?'

'Yes actually, but it isn't a souvenir,' she said wryly.

'Oh,' she said, peering down at her through her thin wire glasses, 'what would that be then?'

'It's my father. He used to live here a long time ago.' The lady carried on rearranging her display at the front of the shop. 'Ah, well I'm afraid I can't help you with that.

You may not find him, but don't let that keep you away from your home,' she said embracing Jasmine's hand. Jasmine picked up some random pieces and handed the shopkeeper a bank note.

'This is too much.'

'It's fine, thank you,' Jasmine replied. Amongst the pieces, patterned scaly skin rubbed against her skin. She looked down to see a coiled toy snake had wrapped its body around her fingers. She walked out knocking the bell above the door. Moisture from the top of the cave dripped down onto Jasmine's neck. She turned around to see where it had fallen from and as her eyes fell back down she glanced through the window at the shopkeeper. She was leaning underneath the till with only her grey hair peeping over the top. Jasmine shook off the snake and threw it as far as she could. She shuddered at the thought; *her grandmother.*

Jasmine had heard her mother banging around that morning, the way she often did when she rushed. She would knock things over and leave behind a trail of destruction like a mini hurricane. Jasmine stood by the door watching her whirl around. It had been a few days since they had heard from her grandmother. The daily phone calls had stopped two days previous and now on this third morning, after failing to reach her, Jasmine's mother began to get ready. 'Are you looking for this?' Jasmine said, her mother's coat swinging casually at her fingertips.

'Yes thank you, darling. I have to go now'

'Will you be long?'

'Perhaps not, I only have to nip and see grandma.'

'Can I come?' Her mother deliberated silently for a moment, Jasmine saw her nod her head ever so slightly that it might have been missed. She followed her downstairs and out into the rain. The SUV was parked on the gravel. They sat in silence together as the window wipers cleared a slosh of rain and then worked ferociously to keep it at bay. Jasmine remembered her grandmother's chats over tea in the sun room. It was Jasmine's favourite part of the house. The slanted glass windows jutted out from the old brick house and created a room made entirely of glass that created a feeling of sitting in the midst of her garden. From the cushioned wicker chairs, Jasmine had a full view of the manicured lawn. The pond was off centre to the right and home to fat, happy frogs and their spawn during the spring. In the winter, it belonged to the snails and slugs that dwelled under stones the same colour as their wet, dark bodies. The trees were trimmed and pruned to within an inch of their life so they had never reached their full potential, they looked wilted in the sun and too cold in the rain. As with everything in the garden, a winding path had been laid with her grandmother's own hands. The path held so much promise touring the garden's delights, it wound past the pond and potted plants, new peonies and seasonal plants, only to end disappointingly at the fence. Her grandmother would interrupt the conversation, always at the same point when the tea was just about cool enough to drink. She would then potter off to the kitchen to bring out the biscuit tin, inviting her to be surprised by its contents. Once she had taken a handful, her grandmother patted her head, satisfied she had pleased her granddaughter and then continued the grown-up talk for that week.

Jasmine didn't remember the exact day it all changed, it was more of a sliding decent. Her usually neat hair became dishevelled around her tired face, her clothes creased and un-ironed, Jasmine wasn't even sure if they were washed. When her grandmother embraced her, she no longer smelt like a starchy washroom and magnolia, but instead of stale, late nights and unwashed bedding. Her voice snorted with incoherent sounds that seemed to escape without warning. Her temper was short. The carpets covering the house were layered with unusual stains, the cushions looked like they hadn't been disturbed in weeks and the sun room windows were smeared with algae and splatters of mud that streaked down the outside. The furniture was pushed to one side and the typically carefully displayed trinkets were pushed to the side of the windowsill with so much force, that most of them lay disfigured on the floor.

'What's wrong with grandma?' Jasmine had asked her mother when it became too obvious to ignore. Her mother had sighed deeply, 'It happens when you get old,' her mother had said. She took another breath as though she was about to say something else but she just stopped. Jasmine didn't think it was that. There was something about the way she acted now that made the change seem almost purposeful. The way she looked over her shoulder when the cats screeched out in the garden, the way she tried to ignore her and her mother's visits as though it pulled her away from something more important. 'Tell me grandmother, what is happening?' Jasmine whispered into her ear when her mother had disappeared on the phone during one visit. 'They are coming for me, Jasmine. I can see them in the night. I can feel them here with me in the empty house.'

'Who?' Her grandmother's eyes flicked from side to side as though they were there; whoever they were, watching and listening for the treacherous words to escape from her lips. But she didn't seem fearful, not yet. She seemed mystified. 'Don't worry Jasmine, they are helping me you see. I was confused and weak but now I am getting stronger. Can you see it in me?'

Jasmine stared blankly at her. All she could see was a dishevelled old woman's descent into madness. Her mother ran in, ending the last conversation she was to have with her grandmother. It was only now, after knowing what lay beyond it, she wondered why her mother had let her go inside by herself that morning. She shivered and focused on the horizon. Her skin started to warm up but the horror wrapped around her heart. 'Here is your change,' said the shopkeeper, exiting the shop.

'Thanks but I didn't want it.' The shopkeeper looked confused and retreated inside. Jasmine knew it was time to leave. An empty cable car had arrived back at the mountain. She opened the door and the porter ran over to lock it behind her. In the grey darkness, her thoughts drifted back to her grandmother.

The door was stiff but unlocked. Jasmine pushed it hard. Stagnant water dripped onto her neck. She walked in and saw the photographs in the hallway. They were hanging off, the glass was broken and smeared so the faces inside them howled through missing mouths and blind eyes. A sharp wind whipped around her and drew her to the kitchen, but it couldn't take away the festering smell that had swamped the place. She imagined the once fat, happy frogs burnt on the cooker and left to rot. The metal sink was ringed with dark stains of red, next to it an electric carving knife was plugged in, a grater was cast aside and pointed metal kebab sticks lay scattered on the floor underneath them. The terracotta pots of plants and herbs were long dead, the soil eaten up by fungus and flies. Jasmine didn't shout out to her grandmother, the house demanded a silent exploration.

The sun room was up ahead. She walked in and her eyes adjusted to the light penetrating the rain streaked windows. Slops of mud clung to the glass and hindered her view to the garden. She could just make out the skeletal figures of the trees in the blank light, darkened by the heaving rain clouds. The pond water was overflowing and forced a black river to roll out over the stones and escape into the garden. Jasmine followed the pool of water with her eyes and found her mind stumbling over how to interpret what she saw; a billow of white fabric, wisps of grey hair, feet the colour of wet stones and the black, hissing creature wrapped around it.

Jasmine's scream was so loud the neighbours had heard it. That's what the police told her at the police station. She heard her mother talking to the officer in the corridor outside. 'But she said she saw a snake there,' her mother whispered.

'There was nothing at the scene, ma'am. A black snake that size would have been spotted in the streets, someone would have seen it or reported it missing. I think it's the trauma of finding her grandmother dead.'

'So, you think she made the whole thing up?'

'Not necessarily made up, but it isn't uncommon in traumatic situations to have your imagination play tricks on you.' Jasmine closed her eyes. She listened to the voices discuss her sanity in the corridors. She saw the scene again and this time the snake smiled at her as it slid away into a dark pit under the ground.

The cable car stopped abruptly at the end. Sounds from the bustle of the wedding party greeted her as she stepped out. Her aunty saw her come through the door and beckoned her over with an eager wave. Jasmine didn't say anything to her about Saeed, she was not even sure what had happened herself. The rest of the wedding and the family greetings passed her by in a blur. By the time they arrived back at the farmhouse, she was relieved to climb into bed. Her body was exhausted but could not rest. The air that stirred into the room through the square hole in the wall brought with it smells of odd beetles and grasshoppers mingled with sweeter notes of night time flowers. Leaving the comfort of her bed she walked outside, willing her mind to take her somewhere new. Her fingers fiddled with the last sealed letter and opened it gently so not to tear, in case it held a secret to something new.

Dear Papa,
Spring, 1948
It has been some years since I arrived in Palestine. I have worked the land as I imagined and lived on my produce. It tastes like nothing else on this earth but I'm afraid it isn't enough for me anymore. By night we speak about Europe. Their war may be over but ours is not

as our fellow men, women and children are dying in the waters trying to get here. They are sent back on ships and the floating dead are found bloated and drifting with the currents. I cannot live peacefully nor enjoy the fruits of my labour when I know this. I have been given a position in the Haganah, a defence force for our people. It is a good job, papa, they pay me a decent wage and soon will provide me with land on which to build. We left milk-churns hidden with explosives in the basement of the hotel where the British Government have their administration quarters. Our assault on the British is one out of many. But it is working. There is talk that the British will leave soon.

I am not a child anymore. I have seen the horrors of war and the atrocities of people. The stories are starting to emerge showing a black stain over Europe and make me fearful of your fate. There is nothing more I can do but pray for you. If there is any chance you are alive then you must come here. It is the place we have often dreamed of.

Yours, Bert.

Jasmine crumpled it up in annoyance. Bert's letters hadn't told her anything. Inside, Miriam's door was ajar. She was asleep on the bed width ways, with her body curled in a semi-circle, her feet tucked up high to escape the chill. Jasmine pulled the door closed, went to the bathroom and washed her face. The water revived her. She looked at her reflection in the mirror and sighed. There was one more man to talk to, if he couldn't provide her with anything then the leads were gone. *'The letters may as well have stayed at home. Maybe I should have too.'*

She went back to her room and lay down on the makeshift bed. A tray with milk and dates had been put on to a wire table next to it. The thick, fleece blanket had been folded up. Uncle Mohammed must have left early to go to the mosque and dropped them in on his way. The milk tasted fresh in her mouth and cooled her throat, the succulent, stuffed dates providing her with comfort to sleep. She lay down on the bed and unfolded the blanket. As her eyes shut, the call to prayer sounded in the distance.

'Come to the good deed, come to the prayer, it is better for you than sleep'. The sounds of the running water coming out of the drains in the homes around her, the shuffling of socked feet in sandals walking to the mosque amidst the darkness and the odd sound of cats calling in the night, filled her thoughts and reminded her of her last visit. It wasn't just the fact she had surprised herself with remembering the translation of the *athan*, or that she remembered the noises at dawn the last time she was with her father in the same house, it was more than that.

A feeling of hope swelled inside her and shook the melancholy away from her body. She missed the faith of her father, the beauty of the dawn streets and the early morning air, the recognition that even in the darkness you were never alone. She had forgotten the blessings bestowed on her. She saw herself over the last ten years and became disappointed. She realised she had wanted for nothing yet did not know gratefulness until she lay under a blanket, gifted from a woman who went to sleep cold for her.

CHAPTER 13

Jasmine opened her eyes the following morning with thoughts of Miriam's kind gestures bringing a smile to her lips. She was interrupted by pots banging from the kitchen, and on entering, found Miriam at the cooker, water boiling away on the stove. 'Can I help?'

'I would like that.' Under Miriam's orders, Jasmine chopped handfuls of vegetables, measured spices and added them to the hot water in the pan. 'That is for the stock,' said Miriam. Miriam then taught her how to wash the chicken in a salt and lemon water mix before Jasmine added it to the stock. Miriam looked satisfied and began to work on the rice grains whilst Jasmine cleared up. 'Would you go and fetch some cucumber and tomatoes for the salad?' said Miriam. So Jasmine wandered out of the back door and through the gardens to the herb garden, where cool air smelling of mint and dried grass tickled her nose. Soon she arrived at the tents, brushed the leaves aside and snapped off juicy cucumbers with their yellow flowers still attached, treading carefully to avoid damaging the family's precious income. She passed into the tomato tent, scooping to pick glossy, red tomatoes from their vine and when her basket was full she ambled back to the house.

The aroma from the kitchen wafted out and greeted her. Miriam had finished frying the cauliflower in spiced oil and was busy adding it to an empty pot with the chicken, stock and rinsed rice. Jasmine washed the stack of pots piling up on the side whilst Miriam polished the saucepans until they shone. When they were packed away into the rickety cupboards, Miriam pulled out a large wooden board. 'It is time to teach you something worth your time now,' said Miriam with a smile.

They rolled out sheets of homemade pastry, thinner than paper, then they pasted on a sticky honey, syrup and butter mixture and added finely chopped nuts before adding more layers of pastry. Jasmine folded up her pastry into odd shaped parcels trying to master the technique, then they placed them side by side on a greased baking tray and lowered them into the oven. Jasmine was exhausted, mostly from the cooking, but it hadn't helped that they laughed until their belly's hurt as Miriam struggled to teach her the refined art of making baklava. Jasmine had barely cooked before and was proud at her attempt at making her favourite sweets. They laughed as Jasmine told of how when she was little she would spy them piled up on a plate inside the meshed larder of her Tata's house and, sneaking a few into the and one of the many hiding places on the farm, she would enjoy every bite before licking the delicious sticky evidence from her hands.

When the midday prayer finished, the family gathered for dinner on the courtyard. Fatima, the widow from next door joined them. Jasmine smiled to herself as she helped Miriam tip the saucepan upside down, the reason to the name of the dish being 'Upside Down' now apparent. They served up browned chicken, rice and cauliflower with blanched almonds, currants and yoghurt. Miriam tossed the salad with lemon juice, freshly picked mint and parsley to accompany it. They sat outside and after praises and utterances of '*Bism'Allah*', Miriam ushered everyone to start eating. Jasmine savoured the warm dish mixed with the crisp, cold salad and the creaminess of the yoghurt, it was delicious and plentiful and a reminder of her love for Arabic food.

Afterwards, when Miriam insisted Jasmine had done enough cleaning, she found her uncle outside in the farm. She was ready to discover Musa's story. Her uncle showed her where he lived, just a few houses away from their farm.

Like most houses on the street, his house was made of stone and concrete well weathered and crumbling. The garden grew out onto the street, clumps of grass clung to life on a slight slope where Jasmine imagined the pavement to have once been. Baby palm trees no higher than her knee sprouted from the ground. Her uncle had explained that most of the locals grew dates to make a living. When she had told him how expensive dates were back in England he just laughed. 'We don't see any of those pounds,' he said. 'We can only sell to the local market. International trade for us was banned years ago.' She wondered how someone could survive selling handfuls of dates. Just then the door opened to a thin, tall man of some age looking hard at her with squinted eyes.

'*Assalam Alaikom*, I am Jasmine Nazheer.' The old man nodded. She recognised him from his younger self in the photograph. 'I was hoping to ask you some questions about my father?' He opened the door wider so she could come inside. She passed a small kitchen and entered the living room. An old TV was pushed up against the wall, a small dining set and stained bark-coloured sofa as old as he was finished off the sparse room. Musa pulled out a hard backed chair and beckoned her to sit. He walked to the kitchen and left her staring at the mottled walls, wondering how her father had felt growing up here in this old city.

Before her first visit, her childish mind had imagined her father's childhood home as a lavish house with grand Middle Eastern décor, turquoise and golden walls, tapestries and carpets lining the halls like a throw-back to the luxurious Ottoman Empire. She imagined hookah pipes lined up on lavish courtyards, men in long robes and black and white chequered headscarves, ladies in black silk dresses covering everything except their faces and hands which dripped with gold. After she visited the reality of Palestine, she had often wondered why they would want to stay in between scrubbed walls with emptiness filling up the spaces.

Musa hobbled back into the room with two glass cups of hot tea. They clinked on the tray. Jasmine stood up quickly and took the tray before the glasses tumbled from his shaking hands. The silence grew awkward. She sipped loudly and winced as the hot tea burnt her lips. 'Your father, he is good man,' said Musa.

'Is there anything you can tell me about what happened to him?' The silence forced her to continue, 'It can be anything at all that you remember. I don't have much to go on.'

'He used to come and sit with the us and write of the conflict between the peoples of Israel and Palestine, here on the borders of our homes and villages. He would give it to the newspapers and keep a record in his red book.' She nodded, her eyes solemn as she remembered her father's writings about Musa's family. It flashed into Musa's greying eyes as though he recalled it with her.

He had been at home with his two sons. The sleepy street awoke to the rolling of heavy wheels on the road, doors slamming as foreign voices shouted menacingly into the night. She saw the trucks outside his windows. She looked at the front door, the scars where it had been re-hinged showed like an old wound sewn up. She saw his young boys being dragged from the beds, clawing at the stone floor, desperate and disorientated, the sound of the gunshot ringing through the air before puncturing the body of his youngest son. She glanced at Musa's older son, then thirteen-year old, in the photograph and the vision of him filled the room. He was heaved into the back of the truck, driven to the jail, hosed down with cold water and left outside in a metal bear cage. The night must have felt like an eternity of torturous contemplation knowing he couldn't help his younger brother. He didn't know that he had died until they released him over three weeks later. Jasmine scuffed the floor with her cork sandal hoping for the noise of it to bring her back to the peace of the present. But down on the floor, rust coloured stains were worn into the grooves of the stone.

'Why do you stay here?' Musa looked at her. Jasmine hadn't meant to say it loud. She disappointed herself for being so tactless. He drew in a deep sigh, as though the answer to the question needed a longer reply than he had the strength for. 'It is our right to fight for our home, our land. If I leave, they win,' he said. He forced the words together so hard Jasmine could see the determination rock his body.

'But it is dangerous isn't it?'

'Death will not escape us whether we try to run or hide from it. It will find us all.' She remembered now why her father had loved his home so much. There was a simplicity and contentment that filled the spaces; a peace that stemmed from the absolute surety that something waited for them in the hereafter that nothing on earth could possess or offer in its favour. That was worth dying for, and worth surviving for. Jasmine thanked Musa for his time and was about to walk onto the street, when she turned back to him in the doorway. 'Do you think I will find him?'

'*Insha'Allah*, as *Allah* wills for only He knows best,' he said and closed the door after her.

Her uncle welcomed her back at the farm. 'There is a march in an hour for our innocent men, women and children. Would you like to come?'

'I was planning on going back to Jerusalem, uncle. There is not much left for me here and there are some things that I need to do before I leave.'

'I will arrange transport for tonight if you want?' A car

pulled up before Jasmine could answer. Its engine droned through the courtyard. 'Aha, your Aunty Khadija is here,' he said.

A heavily pregnant woman clambered out of the car. She rearranged her headdress and pulled her *abaya* so it flowed loosely over her bump. Jasmine recognised her face. She looked older than her years but still held a gracious beauty in her rosy lips and round cheeks. As soon as Khadija saw Jasmine, her face beamed. Jasmine went over to her and introduced herself as Khadija laughed at her formalities. She touched Jasmine's hair and stroked her hand whilst looking intently at her face. 'It is like looking at my mama,' she said, with tears in her eyes.

Jasmine left for the march soon after. She wanted to be there, for her father and for Ali, so she joined the other locals and walked along the streets to a chorus of shouts as they marched towards the nearest army blockade. The streets became alive with hundreds of people unified in their cause for life and justice. Above their heads, they waved posters of the missing, mistreated and the martyrs who had died at the hands of the Occupation.

The Israeli army was expecting them; local journalists had gathered in front of the army's trucks to film the march. Two army trucks parked lengthways across the blockade to prevent anyone passing, young soldiers stood on the ground and others sat in the backs scanning the crowd. They merged together in their camouflage, rifles in hand and sturdy helmets on, ready for war even though faced with an unarmed gathering. Then, Jasmine's eyes were drawn to something. She moved to get a better look and strained her head above the crowds. Her world closed in and spun about her, a laugh she heard before sliced through the air. She needed to get a clear view. She pushed her way through. Her breathing slowed down just enough for her heart to stop pounding in her eyes. There through a gap in the crowds, beyond any doubt, was Josh. He stood side by side with the Israeli soldiers. He was one of them.

Jasmine turned around and weaved through the procession, keeping her head low. Scenarios ran through her mind, remembering how he saved her in the field and why she hadn't understood what he was shouting. She hadn't understood because he spoke in Hebrew, his language and the language of his fellow soldiers. She was his foolish Palestinian informer, his special operation to learn what he could about the enemy, better off alive to him than dead, for now. She felt sick as things fell into place. She remembered the flashlight hanging from his waist as he patrolled outside in the late hours of the night in Betein, his slick routine of checking the house showed training, sharp and efficient. An overwhelming feeling of stupidity and rage surged through her. Her uncle must have seen it. She scanned the crowd for him. He was in danger of being recognised. She was out of her depth with an ignorance she hadn't even realised. Now, Jasmine scrambled to think, what else had she jeopardised in her foolishness?

She ran through the crowds, calling her uncle but it was of no use. She ran back to the farm and stopped for breath as soon as she saw her uncle sitting on the courtyard. He sat forward, a look of concern etched into his face as he saw her approach. 'What is it, Jasmine?' he asked. She couldn't speak. She turned to the street and fled.

She wandered down the old streets steeped in history as she struggled to find her place amongst it all. Her mind tried to work out who else would suffer because of her ignorance. She remembered all the times she had been with Josh. It was his idea to go down into the caves that night. Jasmine wondered what his intention had been taking her down there. Maybe people had been arrested, deported or worse when they found them prowling around the Holy Ground late at night. He had conveniently disappeared and left her. Then, there was the night at the fairground. Jasmine struggled to see through her drunken memory to ask herself what Josh had said to the taxi driver. Then, Betein. She didn't need any more proof.

Without thought, Jasmine found herself climbing the roughed edged stairs cut into the side of Temptation Mountain, the cable car high above her as it vanished over the ledge. She climbed the face with unrelenting resolve, ignoring the burning in her calves, and entered the monastery. She was heading for the ledge outside. She walked through the last door and leant against the railing, looking down into the valley below. Old wounds ripped her insides open. 'Are you alright?' She turned around to face the Priest stood behind her, backing her onto the edge of the precipice. 'What brings you here?'

'I have nowhere else to go.'

'Do you know that you aren't the only one to have sought solace here on this mountain? Jesus did too.'

'Yes, I know the story. It was here he was tempted by the Devil,' she said slowly, trying to end the conversation.

'So you should not be surprised that he would try to tempt you too.' Jasmine felt the tapping begin once more at the back of her skull. 'The Devil can be beaten,' said the Priest, 'but you have to put your soul into the fight.'

'I wasn't going to jump,' said Jasmine, but with each word her cheeks grew hotter.

'You are never alone, dear.'

After a few seconds Jasmine followed him off the balcony, made her way out the monastery and headed down the steps to go home. Her phone rang. It was her Uncle Mohammed. He sounded worried. 'Jasmine, can you come quickly please?'

'What is it, uncle?'

'Khadija, she needs to be taken to the hospital. Something's wrong with the baby.'

Jasmine rushed down the steps and ran back to the farm house. Khadija's skin was pale and damp but she managed to force a smile whilst handing her the keys to her twenty-year-old Audi. Looking at it, Jasmine doubted it would make it to the end of the road, let alone the hospital in Ramallah. Her baby was too premature to risk Jericho's local hospital because of its basic facilities so they headed towards the larger city. After fifteen minutes, Jasmine noticed car lights flashing up ahead. Vehicles were blocking the road. She slowed down as they approached a pop-up checkpoint of crudely placed boulders blocking the road. 'Oh no,' Khadija sighed, breathing deeply. Jasmine wound down the window and showed them her British passport, hoping it would be enough for them to pass.

'And your ID card?' said the soldier gesturing to her aunty.

'I'm taking her to the hospital. She is in labour. We need to get there fast,' said Jasmine.

'There's been a security breach. We can't let you through. You cannot pass here. Try another route,' he said, then turned around and headed back to his truck. Jasmine's blood boiled in anger. She was about to explode. She opened the door to storm after him. 'No, please Jasmine. Leave it. You in prison will be of no help to me tonight,' said Khadija.

'I'll call an ambulance.'

'There's no way it will be here quicker than us driving.' Khadija's breath shortened. She grimaced. 'They don't always let ambulances through either...let us try for Jerusalem.'

'And how long will that take?' Jasmine asked.

'Maybe another half an hour.'

Jasmine knew it was a positive estimate. Aunty Khadija was calm but worry streaked behind her placid exterior. She was used to hiding difficulty, it had been necessary from an early age after both her parents died. Her life became a blur of work and school as she tried to get an education, her dream was to study law when her parents were alive and she would tell them stories of all the things she would do for her country. However, necessity replaced education. At first she helped Mohammed make a living

148

on the farm while studying. The water was drying up, so for months she tried to find ways to recycle water. It was the following spring when the orchard trees started to die. Khadija married Ahmed and left the dying dreams behind to focus on another future; one where she could be a wife and a mother.

A checkpoint outside of Jerusalem loomed into view. Jasmine glanced over at Khadija who was looking into the foot-well, her dress below her knees was damp. She jumped out and ran over to the guards, waving her passport, shouting out the basic human rights she had to get her aunty to a hospital. 'Where is her hospital pass for Jerusalem?' said the guard as he approached the car.

'I did not know I would be needing one. I am not due for weeks. Please, the roads to Ramallah are all blocked.' Khadija replied, but it was of no use. 'No pass, no entry.'

Khadija had told how the Occupation forces increasingly isolated the broken and scattered villages throughout the West Bank, using it as a form of collective punishment to alienate the towns and a means to separate protesting groups from gathering force. Emergencies combined with pop-up checkpoints became un-needed fatalities.

She pulled out her phone. There was only one person to call who might be able to help. 'Josh, its Jasmine. I need your help. My aunty is in labour and we are stuck at the checkpoint just outside of Jerusalem and the soldiers won't let us pass.'

'Thank God you called. I need to talk to you.'

'Are you listening, Josh? I know what you are, Josh. I saw you today. The only hope we have is that we can get to a hospital in Jerusalem, but they won't let us pass through. Can you help or not?'

'I'm on my way.'

Jasmine's hands were clammy as she tried to make her aunty more comfortable. Khadija clasped her hands to her stomach whilst whispering the Quran under her breath.

Headlights appeared on the road behind them. Jasmine's heart dropped when Josh's Jeep screeched to a halt and he jumped out at the checkpoint. He was dressed in his uniform and spoke in Hebrew to the guards manning the checkpoints. He helped Khadija out of the car whilst Jasmine explained to her that he was there to help. She hadn't the energy to protest and smiled painfully in agreement as he helped her into his Jeep. He nodded to the soldiers and they sped off to Jerusalem.

The three of them arrived at the hospital where medical staff rushed out, sat Khadija in a wheelchair and took her inside. Jasmine went to follow, but was collared by the staff to complete admissions forms. Once she had finished, she sat down and burst into tears, relieved she had made it but in a state of shock.

The nurse had told Jasmine how Khadija was one of the lucky ones. She told her of the thirty babies that had died this year alone, after women were forced to deliver by the roadside at checkpoints. In some cases, the mothers had died too. She shuddered imagining the damp-fleshed babies delivered next to the queued cars, limp and turning blue whilst their parents watched them struggle for breath, desperately trying to breathe life into their tiny bodies as they died in front of them. Jasmine felt sick thinking about it and went outside to get some air.

Josh was sat on a bench, staring down into the helmet in his hands. He hadn't seen her. Two women walked past and threw rubbish at his shoes, muttering as they passed him. He didn't flinch. He looked up to see Jasmine, preparing himself for her reproach. 'How are they?' he asked her quietly.

'I don't know yet. Thank you for coming to help,' Jasmine replied shortly.

'Look, Jasmine. I'm sorry I didn't tell you. This isn't…what I am.' She turned her back to walk away. 'Please, Jasmine,' he continued.

Jasmine stopped, allowing him to explain. She owed

him that at least.

'I have to do this work. It is a military state.'

'Everyone has a choice Josh,' she snapped back.

'Yes, everyone has a choice how they treat people, but Military Service isn't a choice for citizens. It's mandatory. Please don't judge me by the uniform. It isn't me. It isn't who I am, it doesn't influence my choices or decisions. I am me, the same person when I am with you.'

'Your military stands for everything I can never be a part of. There isn't anything you can say that will make this better. You totally misled me and compromised my family. You are an Israeli soldier and my family live and die under the Occupation every day.'

He stood up and grabbed her hand pleading with her, he said, 'Not by hands. Never by mine.'

A nurse came outside and approached them. 'You came with Mrs Khadija?' she asked.

'Yes,' Jasmine answered, as she turned back to look at Josh. 'You best go, Josh.'

'Jasmine, I'll prove what I am, give me a chance,' he said.

Without turning back again, she walked off through the hospital doors as he looked on.

'She is asking for you,' said the nurse.

'How is she? How is the baby?'

'*Alhamdullilah* they are both fine,' said the nurse as she led Jasmine into the room where Khadija lay, with a drip in her arm. 'Are you ok?' Jasmine asked quietly, 'How's your baby?'

'She is fine thank you, Jasmine. I have been blessed with a beautiful girl. She is a little tired and underweight, but *Alhamdulillah*, she is good. Thank you, Jasmine. And thank you to your soldier friend.'

Her hands shook as she sat down by the bedside. Jasmine gave her the phone to call her husband. She heard him shriek with delight even from the guest chair. Khadija smiled and spoke gently into the receiver before she hung up. Jasmine sat and gazed out of the window finally relieved but the fear stayed underneath her skin. They are both alive, she kept repeating to herself. But she couldn't stop thinking about those who hadn't made it. The nurse wheeled in an incubator with a tiny baby swaddled in blankets inside. Jasmine walked over and looked through the plastic at Khadija's sleeping baby girl. 'What is her name?'

'Yasmeen,' her mum replied. 'We are going to name her after you, Jasmine.' She thanked Khadija and swiftly excused herself so she wouldn't see her eyes well up. She wandered towards the exit, wondering if Josh would still be outside. On her way out she noticed memorials posted on the wall of the long corridor. Names and dates told stories of those who had died at the hospital. 'Excuse me?' Jasmine said to a passing doctor, 'What is this?'

'When the family are not present, we post their details here.' Jasmine didn't need to hear anything else. She thanked the doctor and began to read the wall. Her stomach churned as she scanned the names one by one. Each time she failed to see 'Nazheer' relief swept over her. The corridor would end soon and she could move on and continue her search for him. Other names skipped by, still hope remained. And then there it was in black and white on the wall, the name resonated with her as clearly as it did from underneath the *'Missing'* photographs she had been handing out all week. *Ibrahim Nazheer'*. It didn't make sense, her family was well known throughout Palestine, they wouldn't have been hard to find. The putrid smell of bleach stung her nose and made her feel sick. She ran towards the door and stumbled out into the clean air and threw up in the bushes. It had never felt as real to her as it did at that moment. Being back in his country made him almost come alive to her once again. 'Are you alright?' a gentle voice spoke to her. Jasmine turned around to see a woman looking at her with concern, 'Is there someone I can call for you?'

'No, there is no one left.'

CHAPTER 14

Jasmine stayed in Jerusalem that night. The old map of Palestine she received from Hiba sat alongside copies of her father's maps, annotated with his handwriting. In both, the same town was marked by a dark ring. It wasn't listed on any of the new maps Jasmine had brought. Some locations disappeared whilst others had had their names changed to Hebrew names. She felt compelled to go and visit, to see for herself the origin of the stories that had shaped not only her family's history but also the country. She wasn't sure if she would ever return to Palestine again and she didn't want to leave any loose ends this time, if she could help it.

At the hotel, she packed her belongings ready to leave and made up a travelling bag with the maps inside it, her mobile phone fully charged and water and snacks. She arranged a rental car from reception. 'Where are you going?' the concierge asked, 'Anywhere nice?'

Jasmine smiled, 'Just to see some historical sites.' She couldn't trust anyone. The rental car arrived and the driver hopped out leaving the engine running. He checked her identification and handed her the keys.

The modernity of the new streets faded once again into

the landscape of hills and olive trees as she left the capital. She drove carefully through the winding roads and glanced at the flat plains below her that had been torn from the mountains side.

She remembered her father, *'On judgement day when the sun is shrouded in darkness, and when the stars lose their light, and when the mountains are made to vanish.'* She imagined the mountains floating in the dark universe and the intensity of her own mortality. Her mother came into her head. Before her death she had often repeated that she had made mistakes about the path she chose in life. She would tell Jasmine how she didn't want her to make the same ones; her soul depended on it. She hadn't understood what her mother was saying at the time but she was starting to now. There was something more that she had believed in once.

She pulled over to the side of the road a few times to check the map. Doubt crept in as she drove. She stuck firm to the sketches on the map and their shared history as if they were both by her side on the journey. Sure enough, the first abandoned village came into view along the roadside, desolate shops standing empty as they echoed her unwanted presence. The sun had bleached posters stuck to the sides of the walls and dust swirled through the village above pot holed roads. She stopped the car to the side of the road and pulled out the map. Her destination was the next village along; the place of her grandmother's birth. She sipped some water, trying to steady her hands on the steering wheel. Releasing the handbrake, she allowed the automatic gear to pull her forward. *'I can't lose my nerve now.'* She pressed down hard on the gas pedal as the car shot to the next village.

Defiant palm trees rooted in the ground which now resembled cracked, matte marble from being damaged by their strength. Their unkempt leaves and old date vine fibres, fluttered like old, bleached rags in the wind. Nature had taken over.

Judging by the maps markings, the old family house

was set back from the street a mile in. She looked at her mileage counter scrolling its way to her destination as fields rolled by the dirt road. The counter ticked. She pressed her foot on the brake and stared at the broken, flat roof home and out-buildings that lay ahead. Her mind flashed back to the remnants of the story she had heard, the rumbling of army trucks approaching from behind her, speeding through the town. Tata, a little girl yet to realise the horrors of man's evil, standing and watching their relentless approach from the house.

Jasmine shuddered, her hands sweating despite the air conditioning blowing loudly. Her foot trembled on the gas pedal, pushing it slowly down to meet her family's fate. She stopped by the side of the road. The path that led down to the house was littered with sharp debris and she didn't want to risk a puncture. She turned off the engine, took a deep breath and stepped out.

She wandered around the ruins of the brick building. Inside the one storey shell that was the home, pots were smashed on the floor like roman ruins, only no one had bothered to piece these back together. A lump of concrete had fallen into a wooden chest crushing all the drawers below it. The roof above it gaped open. She walked into another room, ducking as the door frame hung low to one side under the weight of the collapsing roof. Rusted steel rebar stuck up through the rubble on the floor. She tried to imagine the house whole and alive with the sounds of Tata's ten brothers and sisters running through it and out into the open fields. From toddlers to teenagers, their mother and father all living inside these four walls. She looked down at the old dolls staring up at her torn and blood stained.

A caved in exterior wall led her outside. Rectangular patches of land separated by posts linked with broken wire was overgrown and strangled with weeds. Misshapen lumps of wild vegetables poked up half hidden in the soil making the ground beneath her feet uneven as she stumbled towards the out-houses. Her eyes were brought up from the ground and settled ahead on the remains of the large wooden barn, part hidden by the concrete structures. Her mind recreated the events that unfolded all those years ago, *'She hid beneath the floors of the barn.'* Jasmine's skin bumped with the sinister feeling she had felt when she walked into her English grandmother's house. She pushed away at the debris covering the floor. *'The man stared down at her with his cold green, piercing eyes.'*

Jasmine scraped at the floor now, hoping to uncover the hidden door. She jumped at the sound of a car door slamming in the distance. She moved quicker, frantically searching for the tell-tale sign in the floor, an irrational sense of urgency coursing through her. A sharp nail tore her skin as she turned a metal handle. The door opened upwards revealing a narrow set of stone stairs disappearing into the depths. *'She stayed down there for days.'* She shivered as she walked down the steps into the bottom of the barn and pulled the trap door back over her head.

It was shaded down underneath the floor, shielded from the winds and the cold mountain air that blew through in the winters that the dilapidated barn couldn't avoid. Beneath her feet the remnants of crumbling bone crunched. Above her, footsteps sounded at the entrance to the barn. Dirt fell between the sunlit filled gaps. The figure approached casting a cloud in his path, the sunlight above no longer running down in interrupted streams. She retreated silently backwards to get a better look at the man who was standing above the barn. He kneeled down and peered deep into the shadows of the cellar. In his hand, he held an envelope edged with familiar navy and white striped pattern. His skin was a deathly white, his eyes cold and green as they met hers staring back at him.

***

He had been there before so many years ago and his

157

haunting memories had made it impossible to return until this day. He never found the courage to track the girl he had left alive breathing shallowly under the dead animals and straw. He had tried to pass on his letters to her in the hope that she might forgive him for what he had done. His letters had reached her son but he did not know if they had reached her.

Now in the strangest twist of fate, there she was; beneath the floor boards in the barn as though she hadn't aged a day. The incomprehension dizzied him as he knelt down and stared once again into the almond brown eyes gazing up at him from below the floorboards. They hadn't left his memory since he had looked into them all those years ago. Those big brown eyes filled with loss just stared through him, just like they had done then. It was then he realised that he would never leave this place for a second time. And in the next moment, the girl beneath him took on an ethereal glow, hazy in the broken light that streamed through the barn floor. Her own inner light beamed from beneath her skin. 'Forgive me', he mouthed to her as she barely breathed under the barn floor. He looked up as the light slowly changed, a dark shape clouding the sky. Sunlight no longer shone through as an other-worldly Being appeared, its enormous figure filling all remnants of light with darkness. The Angel of Death had come for his soul.

**

It took Jasmine a few minutes to understand what was happening. The figure above had clutched at his heart, grimacing as he fell to his knees with his green eyes fixated on her. She ran up the stairs, the barn door swung open and a silhouetted figure ran towards them. The old man writhed on the floor, his lips beginning to turn grey with the signs of death already taking over him. 'Jasmine, what's happened? Grandpa, can you hear me?'

She backed off, *'Grandpa'* Seconds ticked by, as slow as an eternity, before her body snapped into the automatic response of the emergency. 'Shall I call an ambulance?'

'It will never find us here. We need to get him in the car. Stay with him whilst I bring the Jeep closer.' Josh ran off before she had time to protest. She didn't know what to do. The old man gasped for air but still didn't take his eyes off hers. She knew he was dying but she was more terrified that sharing the same air would mean she would die. She was the same with her mother, the smell of approaching death, the irrational thoughts of it being airborne contagion. His thin strands of white hair barely covered his brown spotted scalp. She wanted to reach for his hand to provide him with some comfort but her body was in turmoil. *'How could she comfort this man?'* She stepped back and watched from a slight distance, shocked and emotionally removed as if she was watching a struggling animal. The thought of smashing him over the head with a stone came into her head, just as she had done with the hyena. She took a deep breath and was relieved to have her thoughts broken by the sound of Josh's Jeep skidding to a halt outside the barn.

Jasmine stayed where she was, watching Josh carry him and lift him into the Jeep. He struggled slightly, not because of the weight but because of the awkwardness of trying to fold his grandfather's long body and legs gently into the backseat. Josh pushed back the passenger seat, sweat falling from his forehead. He wiped it away with his sleeve and looked at her. Jasmine stared into his green eyes. She turned away. 'Come on Jasmine, we have to go.' She wanted to say no, to tell him to stay away but she opened her mouth and no words came out. She tried to stand on her feet but her legs buckled underneath her.

'Jasmine, you are in shock, it's Ok. Come on let me help you, you need to come with me.' He lifted her arm and wrapped it round his shoulder, his strength guiding her to the Jeep. She sat in the front seat and looked into the mirror. It reflected the old man as he lay dying. The soul through his eyes begged to stay alive, but she knew it was a battle he would lose. Josh rammed the Jeep into gear and sped off up the winding road. Jasmine turned outwards to the barn and house, at her new rental car sharply offsetting the balance of the abandoned ruins. The village turned into a blur of dust and memories as they raced through it. When she looked at Josh, all logic melted away despite knowing that betrayal and division sat behind them, between them and undoubtedly, ahead of them too.

CHAPTER 15

Josh swung the Jeep into a space outside the Accident and Emergency door. Paramedics rushed out and helped lift his grandpa onto a stretcher. An oxygen mask was placed over his mouth. She watched Josh, in control again, as he gave them an account of what happened. But he didn't know the whole truth, not without the letters. She took them from her bag and placed them on the back seat. Josh approached her slowly and climbed in.

'How did you know where to find me?'

'You told me.'

'Did I?' Jasmine thought, but she was too shocked to question it. 'I will go and park, you go with him. I'll leave the keys under the wheel,' she said, changing the subject.

'Are you sure?'

'Yes, go be with him.'

He got back out of the Jeep. Then he stopped and turned around, 'Will I see you again?'

'I am not sure that's a good idea,' she said.

'Please, Jasmine. I will make it possible for us to have a future. Trust me. I am not what you think.' She nodded, but she knew from the sadness in his eyes he didn't trust her response. 'Josh, you need to go.'

Jasmine turned the Jeep around, the steering wheel warm from his palms, his scent still lingering. Turning her head to reverse the car, she looked down at the pile of opened letters, the true extent of their secrets now exposed. Her attention was drawn to a sealed letter protruding up from the corner of the back seat, crumpled from the old man's fist. She ironed it out with her palm, slid her finger under the old seal and read Bert's final piece.

Dear Papa,

Our son was born in the spring of 1950. It should have been a time of celebration but the spring day was too similar to another such day which has now altered my life forever. This is my confession papa, but I do not think any amount of regret can give me respite from what I will face when I die. It was not just fate that I had remembered it then. I stood at the end of the hospital bed, unable to hold my new-born son. His cry induced my body to shake as it unlocked a door into my subconscious, to the scene of my ultimate crime. It was another day, another place, where a baby wailed in its mother's arms whilst it's mother lay dead still cradling him. Another slice from the cold blade ripped through soft flesh and its crying stopped.

It was April 1948 when we attacked the village. At first we used stealth, the silence and the brutality of knives. It was personal and close yet we found ourselves void of emotion. Only now am I haunted by my own brutality. I could barely see through the blood mist covering my eyes. We stormed house after house where children cowered beneath sparse units, unable to hide, their parents defending them hopelessly against our onslaught. Afterwards, I went to the final place. It was there that I was looking through the barn floor into the eyes of a young girl as she cowered beneath the straw. Her eyes gave me a glimpse at the surety of retribution that will follow me forever, so I left her there, alive.

In the time that followed, on the streets of Jerusalem, a young girl would see my soul with those same eyes. A group of teenagers would be smoking around the walls of the City. One of them would turn and stare through me with those dark, accusing eyes. Any one of them could have been her. I want to find her and give her my letters so that by some small chance, she can understand my reasons. I pray for forgiveness in the hope that when I die, I might be saved from the punishment of my sins.

Yours, Bert.

The confession confirmed what she already knew. Her father must have kept them away from her Tata and for good reason, but with both of them gone she would never know for sure if her Tata had ever read them. She looked up from the letter at the hospital. It was the place her father's body had been confirmed dead, the place where she could get the documents she needed for her inheritance; the money, the house, her future. She needed to move forward, to release her father. She needed to collect his death certificate. Her mind tried with difficulty to recreate her English dream but it felt wrong. She pushed the thoughts aside and let her legs carry her burdened body out of the car. The nurse stood behind the stark white of the reception desk and smiled at her. 'Hi, I need a death certificate. Could you tell me where to apply, please?' said Jasmine.

'I can help you my dear. What name is it?'

'Ibrahim Nazheer.' His name was on the wall but the formality of the proceedings made it feel real. It would give her closure in more ways than one, yet grief washed over her with the realisation of both parents' death within days of each other. The nurse clicked the buttons on the computer, unaware of the inner turmoil in front of her. 'I am sorry. We don't have anyone by that name registered. Was he pronounced dead by a doctor here?'

'Not exactly. I saw his name on the memorial wall in the corridor,' said Jasmine, pointing in its direction.

'I am sorry dear; did no one explain?' Jasmine shook her head in bewilderment. 'In these cases death certificates cannot be issued from here because we cannot be certain of their identities.'

'But it said his name, a date.'

'I'm sorry. It is just one of those unfortunate things. We are given information however in those cases when it cannot be confirmed by a family member in time, the body is buried.'

Jasmine's voice croaked unwillingly, 'What am I supposed to do now? I can't find him anywhere, I can't have a death certificate, what do you expect me to do?' Her tears started to fall.

'Where was your father born?'

'In Jericho,' Jasmine sniffed.

'Well, they will probably issue you one there. But you need to go to Jericho to file for it.'

She walked away from reception, planning out her next moves. First, she needed to collect some things from the hotel and call the rental car company to go and collect the car she had abandoned in the village, she knew she wasn't going to go back there. She passed the waiting room where Josh stood leaning into the coffee machine. His eyes were red and his fingers pulled at the empty plastic cup. All the logic and reasoning disappeared. She ran over and wrapped her arms around him. They didn't exchange a single word, nothing needed to be said and no words could explain it all. A grieving family walked into the room echoing the sobs she felt rise from her body. Reluctantly, Jasmine let her arms fall and whispered goodbye.

***

'Jasmine?' the voice repeated her name several times before it penetrated through to her subconscious. 'Josh?' Her eyes opened to a familiar face. 'Uncle?' She half smiled and closed her eyes again embarrassed at what she had said. When she reopened them, he was there by her side. The familiarity of their home in Jericho filled the tidy room. The walls held the scent of deep spices and the bed smelt of freshly washed linen and Miriam's flowery perfume. It welcomed her.

'What happened?' she asked.

'You fainted at the hospital. You must be exhausted; you look like you haven't been sleeping enough.' Her last memory was Josh so she changed tact. 'Khadija and her baby are fine.'

'*Alhamdulillah*, but I knew that, Jasmine. We had just visited her when we found you in the corridor. Are you ok?' His soft way of extracting information was always unavoidable.

'I followed the last story there was, uncle.' He frowned. Jasmine took it as confusion so she carried on, 'I know what happened to Tata, so I went to find the village on an old map and I found, well…Josh, he is…not what I thought.'

'Ah, your soldier.'

'How did you know?'

'Of course, it is obvious to me, Jasmine, but it was your story to discover. *Allah* has his plans for us all.' Jasmine couldn't believe there was no argument. She wanted a response, some shock so she blurted out her other discovery. 'My father is dead.'

'How do you know that?'

'In the hospital, his name was on a memorial on the wall.'

'Anyone can put names on that wall. It's nothing but propaganda. It proves nothing.'

'I am going to the registry office to collect a death certificate before I leave. I need it for my inheritance.'

'A death certificate will not be any more conclusive.'

'Then what do you suggest, uncle? That I spend my life searching for him? That I lose everything that he worked for?'

'I think you need to understand what you should be living for. That is more important.' He walked away with his hands behind his back. Jasmine left the farm house and walked briskly to the government offices in town. She scrawled the application form for her father's death certificate and waited outside impatiently for it to be processed, flitting between stalls and shops. Her search was over. This was the last thing to tick off and she could go home. There was no father to find anymore. After this she would head straight to Jerusalem, pack up her things and leave. A vision of her home floated into her head but even that seemed unreal. She couldn't imagine walking through the bare halls stripped of her mother and it feeling like it was home. She walked back into the administration office. The teller called her over and handed her an envelope. She opened it up and read the confirmation she had needed. But closure still escaped her. She called the solicitors from the payphone on a quiet part of the street. 'Smith and Holdson Solicitors, how can I help?'

'My name is Jasmine Nazheer. Can I speak to Henry? He is dealing with my mother's probate.'

'Hold on a moment.'

'Hello,' a man's voice picked up the line. 'How can I help?'

'Henry, it is Jasmine. I have my father's death certificate. Is that all I need?'

'I hoped I didn't have to tell you this over the phone, Miss Nazheer but there has been another claim on your mother's Estate.'

'What? What do you mean?'

'Richard Banbury has filed a claim for the inheritance as well.'

'That doesn't make any sense. How can he do that? I am her daughter, who is he? Nobody!'

'I suggest you travel back as soon as possible and we can take it from there.'

'Don't do anything without me, I mean it, nothing.'

'Of course,' said Henry formally. Jasmine hung up and screamed out loud, startling two passers-by. She ran back to her uncle's house. Her inheritance, her money to build the life she dreamed of from the depth of her mother's illness was slipping away from her. The hope of her father had died the moment the ink was printed onto his death certificate and even Josh stood on the opposite side of the security fence.

Jasmine contemplated a future she had no idea how to live, wandering around the ruins of the farm, avoiding the humid cucumber tents and hopping over dead orchard stumps, seeking refuge to collect her thoughts. Unfamiliar faces walked past the farm, she heard her aunty and uncle conversing in private. All she could make out was that movement from the Israeli bases had picked up and the streets were quieter than usual. It was time for her to leave before doing any more damage. 'I'm ready to go, uncle.'

'A soldier's gone missing. Do you know anything about it, Jasmine?'

'No uncle.'

'Where did you get this?' he said, changing the conversation and twisting the rope of the bracelet wound tightly on Jasmine's wrist.

'A necklace seller gave it to me. For protection,' she answered.

Her uncle's voice changed. His undertone was sharp and serious, 'Nothing can provide you with protection except *Allah* Himself. This is *haram*, please get rid of it.' She nodded and unwound the bracelet from her wrist and tossed it into the smouldering fire. The distorted eyes melted into lumps of plastic and toxic fumes. Jasmine said her goodbyes to Miriam and climbed into her Uncle's borrowed, tattered car. She waved to her tearful aunty out of the window, the choking feeling worming its way into her throat. The car pulled off and in the uncomfortable silence, as Jasmine dwelled on the missing soldier, Mohammed whispered the Quran under his breath. As they approached the road border out of Jericho, she noticed an unusual amount of lights flashing ahead. 'What is it uncle?' she asked.

'They have closed the checkpoint. No one will be

leaving now.'

Jasmine spent the next day in the back of the garden, away from the sound of the tanks rumbling past the old houses. Sometimes she peered from the back of the house in the hope of seeing Josh on one of the military vehicles. The streets were littered with more people than usual, all heading for the town centre. Ignoring her uncle's advice, she followed them, walking past empty courtyards and closed shops.

A crowd jostled in the square, shouting and waving Palestinian flags. The army tanks crawled around the perimeter. A soldier looked at her incriminatingly as he spoke into his radio. She pushed herself deeper into the crowd and pulled her headscarf over her nose and mouth so only her eyes were visible. Beneath the veil, she looked around nervously but she couldn't see anything except bodies in the crowd. The air became thick and she could hear the sound of her heart hammering in her ears again. She pushed her way through and took off her veil, breathing lungful's of air on the edge of the crowds, trying to stave off a panic attack.

'Traitor!' a teenager's voice shouted. Someone ran towards her for a better look. The man shouted in Arabic and was joined by three others. A woman grabbed her arm, 'Go, Nazheer, go back to your Uncle's.' Jasmine rushed down the street and away from the crowds back towards her uncle's farm. She had not noticed the teenagers following behind her. 'You brought him here,' shouted one of them as they caught up with her 'you bought the soldier.' She kept walking until they circled her at the bottom of the street. 'Traitor, do you know we kill traitors like you.'

'I am not, I wouldn't…' said Jasmine, trying to get her words out. 'They've seen us,' she said pointing over their shoulders. It didn't elicit a response so she grabbed one of their faces and pushed it around at the soldiers heading towards them. They fled, Jasmine turned and ran too, the sound of thuds echoing on the pavement. She arrived at her uncle's house breathless, panic streaking through her eyes. 'What is it?'

'They're coming,' she gasped out between breaths. 'The soldiers have seen me. They know, they all know.' Miriam rushed inside and collected her bag. She returned with tears in her eyes and shaking hands. She kissed her and whispered Arabic over her head whilst her uncle spoke. 'Go to Temptation Mountain. Look for the escape. It's the only way you can leave now.'

'But uncle, how will I find it? I cannot leave you both, it is too dangerous.'

'Go!' he shouted, '*Allah* has his own plan for us.'

Jasmine ran hard down the street keeping close to the houses. When the street was empty, she darted into the fields. The dry earth crunched beneath her feet and her legs felt heavy under the black material wrapping itself around her legs. Tanks rumbled by the roads that surrounded the fields. Beyond the roads lay the base of the mountain. Two soldiers paced up and down the road, checking cars as they passed. Jasmine had no choice but to walk out into the road, she whispered to herself, '*Bism'Allah*' and hoped to God they would be distracted elsewhere. She took a deep breath to try and stop her legs from shaking and wiped the sweat from her face. She focused ahead on the base of the mountain and stepped out into the road.

One after another, she crossed the short distances, praying as she went that she wouldn't be stopped. She slipped between the banana tree plantations and out of view from the roadside, approaching Temptation Mount. She couldn't rest yet. She had no choice but to climb the mountain. Step after step, she heaved herself up its face, following the trodden path the Christian pilgrims had worn into its side.

Half way up, the dark terrace welcomed and concealed her. She lay on the deck exhausted. The place was deserted. The cable cars were motionless. Chairs were stacked up neatly against the wall, the bar and restaurant empty. She opened a fridge and grabbed a couple of bottles of water, leaving money on the bar. Drinking as she walked, she headed for the monastery.

The door was open and she followed the excavated corridor once again, desperately trying to find something that might give her clue as to what Mohammed had spoken of. The monk's doors were locked and no one was inside. She reached the interior room at the back of the cave where the paintings looked down at her in pity. She pushed parts of the wall. Nothing.

She went outside to the ledge, turning away from the inviting fall so she wasn't staring down as she had done before. She was almost about to give up when she remembered, Saeed. She walked over to where he had disappeared. She slumped down and leant into in the corner. Beneath her fingers she felt something scratched into floor. It was Arabic writing. She scored over the letters with her finger. The calligraphy was familiar. She didn't know what it translated to but she recognised the pattern.

A whisper of a word whistled by her ear startling her. She panicked and knocked her elbow into the wall behind her. She winced in pain before clasping her hand over her mouth. Then she felt it; a thin stream of air against her hand coming from the wall. She moved from where she was sitting and pushed. A block separated and moved inwards to reveal an opening leading down into the darkness.

CHAPTER 16 JOSH PART 3

Jasmine had gone. He had placed her limp body in the chair with the nurses looking over her, and watched from behind the door as her uncle lifted her out of the hospital. When Josh made it back to his grandfather's bedside he saw the old man's toes curled up as if broken, his head jutted backwards with eyes wide and tortured staring up at the ceiling. Josh shouted the doctors in, 'How long has he been like this?' he demanded, but they passed on their condolences, there was nothing they could do. They pulled the curtain closed and allowed him some time to say goodbye.

He tried to close his grandfather's eyelids and adjust his body to become more relaxed, to resemble a peaceful sleep, but the body cracked and moaned with every movement. His eyelids dropped down slightly but would not fully close, revealing strips of ghostly white beneath his grey lashes. Josh didn't need to be told that he died of a massive heart attack. He had guessed as much at the sight of his hands grasping at his chest. The remaining pieces of his life were now stitched together by his own handwriting in a pile of letters.

A closed casket was the only option for his funeral.

Josh couldn't bear to see the old man's final moments forever etched into his face. It didn't matter anyway, there was no-one left to decide otherwise. He paid his respects by carrying the coffin to the bed of the grave with assistance from the pall bearers at the funeral house. They lowered it into the ground as the Rabbi conducted the service. The repetition of God's mercy rang out into Josh's ears. He burnt the letters and scattered the ashes on top of the coffin. Soil lay in heaps either side of the hole. Josh shovelled the soil and began to bury his grandfather with all that was left of his life in this world; bones, deeds and the dust of his memoirs. Josh thought of his future, of Jasmine and the land he was burying his grandfather in. The Rabbi had left. The stray mourners from the funeral home patted Josh on the shoulder and left him kneeling in the dirt staring down into the soil. No tears fell. He glanced at his watch. It was time to go. He stood up, whispered something over the soil and walked away.

***

The Jeep tore through the desert, the sand whipping around its wheels and the sun baking it's exterior. As the desert sand flattened and the GPS flashed a straight red line, he slowed down. His thoughts came away from his destination and instead saw Jasmine. Her face seemed to shape into the clouds above his head and in the ever changing curls of sand that were delicately blown across the desert floor in the distance. He tried to stop the idea but it formed in his head. He remembered the way she looked at him now. She probably didn't notice it herself, he thought, but the change simmered behind her illuminated brown eyes. He wondered where she was now, what she was thinking. Would he even find her after this? He ragged his steering wheel to the left and almost toppled the Jeep. Ahead of him, the place he had been trying to get to dissipated into the air under the shimmering heat, as though it was a mirage. He stamped on the gas and felt the wheel's spin underneath him. It took all his skill not to get stuck in the sand.

The dense, concrete walls appeared after over two hours of driving through the desert. He had pinpointed his destination on a map in case his GPS failed; prepared as always. The prison loomed over its terrain with high walls ringed with barb wire, its four corner posts manned with armed soldiers twenty hours a day. He was travelling under the pretence of having orders to look for an escaped prisoner. He needed access to the prison to help in providing documents to assess the case. He tried to find weaknesses in his alibi. An escape from the Fortress looked almost impossible if it went wrong. So did Alcatraz though, he thought as he repeated the plan over and over. He switched off his phone, slowed down on the approach to the gates and pressed the entry button. CCTV twisted round to face him. The crackling sound stopped. Someone was listening on the other side. 'Josh Bergman, I am here to see Mr Havron.' He held his ID open to the camera. The buzzer sounded to release the gate as he drove through into the heart of the prison.

Havron was one of the senior officers in charge. Josh kept his conversation brief. 'There has been a leak about a prisoner escaping. I am here following protocol. I need access to your documentation room.' When Havron interrogated the reasons further and asked where the information had come from, Josh declined to divulge based on protection of national interest. 'Very well. I will ask a guard to escort you to the documentation room and then if you will excuse me, I have business to attend to and must get on my way.'

'Of course,' said Josh, following Havron out into a stairwell. An elevator took the three of them into a basement. 'Records,' Havron said, as he unlocked the door and led Josh into the lit windowless room. Corridors of heavy, gun metal shelving units lined the floor, weighed down with countless files listed in alphabetical order. 'Thank you,' Josh replied. Havron nodded and left him to it. Josh found a step-ladder at the side of the room and went straight to the files. He pulled the first stack of documents and hauled boxes back up onto the shelves. The guard approached him offering help, looking into the boxes inquisitively at the names. Josh spoke to him sharply, 'This is top secret and of national interest officer so if you want to jeopardize your position and risk treason feel free.' The guard turned quickly and returned to his position at the door, watching him intently.

Amongst the papers and khaki files, a name started to form in front of his eyes. He opened the file and read the contents, scanning quickly for the pieces of information he needed. The guard came over once again. Josh slid the file back in and grabbed another one out before the guard had a chance to peer over his shoulder. 'I am done now. We can go,' said Josh, interrupting the guard's conversation on his radio. As they exited the lift Josh followed the guard as he took him in a different direction from the way they had entered. 'Where are we going?'

'Just come with me,' was the guards reply. Josh furiously scanned around for exit routes. He was surrounded by iron bars that rose from the floor to the ceilings, broken up by manned gates and watched by CCTV. The guard opened a door into the back of an interview room, 'Havron will be with you soon. Wait here please.' A large one-way mirror was set into the wall in front of him, allowing him a view of a plain room with a desk and two chairs. Handcuffs were hard fixed to the top of the steel desk. To his left a bank of CCTV screens displayed high resolution images of children huddled together inside claustrophobic prison cells. Their faces were grubby and marked in cuts and the sound that scraped through the speakers was of coughs and whispers behind small hands. Josh stared at the screens. He peered closer. His fists curled on the table as the images switched back and forth across the cell floors. He knew what he was capable of. His mind's eye tempted him with a vision of rage that he felt well within his capabilities. His thoughts came back sharply to his current predicament as he heard the zoom of the camera on the wall above him. He allowed his fists to uncurl, his back straightened up. He looked up to face the camera and sat on the chair in front of the screens. He swung his legs up nonchalantly. As always it was a matter of timing, he thought. At that moment the door unlocked and Havron walked in.

'Business was cancelled then?' asked Josh.

'Pass me the file.' Josh handed it to him. Havron opened it and studied the contents. He spoke into his radio and waited for a response. Havron gestured at the CCTV, 'We have to watch these terrorists. They are getting younger every year.'

Josh moved his head and glanced back to Havron. 'What are they in for?'

'Acts of terror. Stone throwing has a five-year sentence now. We are filling up quickly,' he smirked.

Josh's memory played back to a patrol a few months back. It was rocks they threw at the army truck that afternoon. It didn't even scratch the metal of the hulk. He knew this was a test. He kept quiet and allowed Havron to await the return on the radio. A one-word response came through and broke the building silence. Josh could see from Havron's altered breathing pattern, and the slight shift in his stance that it was an answer Havron was happy with. 'You can go,' he said immediately afterwards. Josh swung his legs down from the chair. As Havron unlocked the door, he placed a firm hand on Josh's shoulder, 'We have to always air on the side of extreme caution.' Josh sloped his shoulder to get the hand off and allowed himself to be escorted off the prison grounds.

Havron had gone but as he walked through the corridors Josh caught a reflection of him through the security mirrors; he was talking into his radio, screening his lip movements with his hands. The guards changed position by the exit gates. Their numbers seemed to have doubled. They stood attentively, watching him closely as he forced his body to relax. Josh glanced back at their faces and saw the uneasy tension ripple beyond their irises as they waited for orders. He had seen it many times, usually before an attack. He climbed into his Jeep, started the engine and left the boundaries of the prison.

His eyes glanced back and forth between the rear view mirror and the openness of the expanse of sand ahead. Nothing stirred in the sands behind him besides his own trail. He drove on as the sun began its descent. He knew the desert would be ending soon and he would be back reunited with civilisation on its borders. With that in mind and the prison now separated by miles of sand, he began to see Jasmine again. He saw her in the sands and her voice whispered to him reinforcing his mission, his new purpose. Even the fading light didn't darken his thoughts. The sun became an orange half-moon, sinking into the earth. The sky above it was striped with rose and amber and turned the shapes of distant mountains into shadows. The sands whistled louder through the gaps in his window. The air had picked up, the slight change in vibrations underneath his wheels told him something else was sharing the land. He glanced into his rear view mirror; a dust trail whirled above a flash of light. He held his hand out of the window and slowed down the car. Some-thing was trailing behind him, desperate to catch up. He slammed his foot down on the accelerator and sped towards the horizon.

CHAPTER 17

Jasmine slid her body down into the hole and closed the gap above her head. Her feet found their way down the tunnel in the pitch black. A wall compelled her to stop and turn as a pinholes of light emanating from the roof reached her in the dark and illuminated just enough to see the stone staircase spiralling down. A passage opened out at the bottom, a narrow corridor leading her into more darkness.

After hours of walking blind with nothing but her hands to guide her along the rough stone wall, she saw light seep into the passage and scatter through the gaps, dappling onto the walls of the cave revealing the way out. She pushed through the thorny bush and made her way towards the empty road wondering how far she was to Jerusalem. She turned around and glanced back at the mountains she had just passed underneath and already the entrance to the cave had disappeared. An old car chugged out white smoke by the side of the road. A man wearing a black and white *keffiyeh* scarf slept with his feet up on the dashboard. He jumped awake at the sound of her passing and scrambled out of the car. 'Wait, wait' he shouted. Jasmine halted, too tired to protest or run. He was an elderly man, almost non-threatening, with a well-worn *dishdasha* and holes in his shoes. 'Miss Nazheer, come with me. I am from your uncle. Come quickly.'

'Who else would have known I would be here?' she thought to herself as she climbed into the car. He handed her a bottle of water and pulled out an old Nokia phone. He pressed redial and spoke in Arabic. She was relieved to hear uncle's voice on the other end. 'Jerusalem?' the old man said. Jasmine nodded her head and sank back into her seat.

He dropped her off just outside the checkpoints. She passed through unscathed with her British passport and jumped into a waiting taxi and headed back to her hotel. Once she had arrived, she walked through the lobby doors, dishevelled and exhausted. The concierge called her from the reception desk. 'We have a parcel that was left for you here.'

'Who is it from? When did it arrive?' Jasmine asked, but the concierge just stared at her with a blank smile. The parcel was handed over and she opened it, holding her breath. Inside was a hospital card with a Jerusalem address and scrawled in blue pen on the front was the name, *'Mr Mansour'.*

Her brain fought with her heart. She wanted to leave, to go to the airport and head back home to claim what was hers, but her heart desperately wanted to find Josh. She went to her room and tossed the hospital card on the bed. She shoved her things into her suitcase, opened drawers, looked underneath the bed and scanned around the room to double check she hadn't left anything behind. She sat on the floor with her head in her hands, knowing she couldn't go through another decade suffering the uncertainty of what could have been. She left her packing and ran outside to flag down a taxi with the hospital card held tight in her hand.

At the hospital reception she lied and told how she was a relative of Mr Mansour. She was shown onto a ward where a blue curtain hid everything except for the sound of steady breathing and the slow, rhythmic beep of machines. They reminded her of the hospital visits back in England and filled her with dread. She turned away to walk off. She couldn't deal with anymore loss, anymore pain. 'This way,' the nurse said and guided her back, opening up the curtain to reveal a man lying on the hospital bed. Her mind reflected the same postured form so familiar to her; to a place and time removed from the present, as he lay in their bed.

The bed was her mother's, the morning sunlight penetrated the gaps in the curtains and fell upon the profile of his strong face. Eyes were hidden under closed, furrowed brows, the ones she was looking at now were reflected in her memory and almost identical. Intrepidly, she moved forward to a hand dangling from the bed. She picked it up in hers and closed her eyes. It was a hand she had once held often, a hand that guided her and comforted her.

The figure turned his head to her. His eyes opened. They looked at her with shock, sadness and hope all at once. His face rolled into the pillow to blot away the tears. The smell of burnt golden grass and English fields filled the room as if they had just returned from watching the sunset together like they had done all those years ago. It was as if time had not passed in years but in lost moments.

'I thought you were dead.'

'You weren't to know.' He said softly, easing her through.

'I didn't try and find you, I'm so sorry. I thought you left. I thought you didn't care about us anymore.'

'You were only a child then, *habibte*.'

'Mother knew didn't she?'

'She suspected I was still alive. But no one knew for sure.'

'She said you could help her. That you knew the answers, but she was slipping away, losing her mind.'

'No, Jasmine. She didn't want you to grow up missing

out on what you need.' His words resounded in her head. She saw it now. The love her mother had for her was worth more than all the money in the world. Her mind flashed back to the last nights with her. Jasmine had heard the butterfly's wing fluttering in the darkness and now she understood. It was the sound of her mother turning the wafer thin pages of the Quran that was missing from the soft dust bag in her father's things, the incoherent mumbling was her recitation of Arabic, conversing in private with a sense of dying urgency. *That is why she left the light on.'* Her mother had loved her enough to send her to Palestine to discover what her soul yearned for.

After some time, Jasmine went out into the corridor to make a phone call. She called the solicitors office and arranged for the forms to be faxed over to the hospital for her father's countersignature. The solicitor called her back within minutes to let her know Richard had withdrawn his counter claim now her father was alive. The inheritance was hers, but it was no longer what she lived for.

Back by his bedside, Ibrahim told his daughter the story of what had happened all those nights ago and she imagined the scenario unfold as he spoke. After Ali was shot, Jasmine's mother flew out to Palestine to bring her back to England, she was furious with Ibrahim for putting their daughter's life at risk. She vowed that she would never again let her travel to Palestine. When they arrived home, her father and mother had argued relentlessly. She cried. He left, telling her about the justice he wanted for Ali, for the locals. He had to return. 'Is that why you were arrested?' she asked.

'No, *habibte.* I was taken from the field behind the house in Betein. Ali's brother, Adam, planned to seek revenge there on the soldier that shot his brother but I saw him that night. I watched him sneak into the field and I followed him.' Jasmine knew the rest. She had seen it herself, the silhouettes of frog-like men in camouflage near the hilltop. She imagined her father grabbing Adam and holding him down out of sight of Ali's killer. 'What did you say to him that made him change his mind, father?' Jasmine asked, holding his hand as she sat by his bedside.

'I told him a verse from the Quran, one we should live by. It translates to: *To kill one person is equal to killing the whole of humanity, to save one life, is equal to the saving of humanity.*' Such is the forgiveness and peace of true faith. It must have resonated with Adam because he agreed he would wait for true justice to be done but that was not our fate. Like shadows in the night they seized us and we were taken somewhere remote. I was kept in the dark and isolated for months before being transferred to prison. I never heard from anyone again.'

'How did you get out?'

'There was someone in the prison, I cannot tell you who it was but he knew of me, he knew of us Jasmine. He told me someone from the inside had arranged for my freedom and he hinted that the press was onto my case.'

'Why would that matter?' Jasmine asked.

'I have been imprisoned for over ten years now without trial and with the pressure the country is under, they don't need cases like mine being under the spotlight, it only incites revenge attacks. Our family is a big family my dear and the shockwaves are far greater with our family influence. Someone must have leaked my documents showing who I was and that I was still alive. It was enough.'

Jasmine's mind worked furiously. *Would they ever find who it was her father was talking about? Did it matter?* Of course she had a feeling she already knew. Her father squeezed her hand. 'My only prayer was to see you again, Jasmine. You see how *Allah* loves us?' She squeezed his hand back. 'He brought you here back to me, back to Him. We are truly blessed.'

***

Later that year, there was still no news about Josh. Back in London the winter brought with it cold rain. The memories of her mother sweetened and eventually the years they had lived together overshadowed the final moments which had previously tainted her dreams.

When Jasmine's father had recuperated enough he went back to the farm. He called Jasmine often and told her how he had prepared the land, tore out the stumps and tilled the soil until it was ready for the seeds; he was planting a lemon and orange orchard in his mother's once beloved garden. She knew he did it for Khadija too. He told Jasmine how he hoped to build an apartment for Khadija and her family in the grounds of their farm in Jericho, how Khadija now planned to go to university to study law and Miriam was delighted at the thought of tending to a baby who belonged to the closest person she had ever had for a daughter. She imagined Jericho and the farm in bloom once again. Sometimes, she imagined she heard the *athan*. It seemed to float around her briefly before drifting away.

Life in London grew stale. She longed for the richness and discoveries that lay in her father's homeland. She had so much more to learn there. Josh was there and alive too, she felt it in her bones and her dreams of him hadn't subsided. 'Come and live here with me, Jasmine?' her father asked the following summer.

From that moment, everything fell into place. She arranged to live with her father back in Jericho. When she arrived, it was better than she had imagined. The *athan* resonated in the air and structured their days around the prayer. She would occupy the afternoons in cool, musk-scented mosques that provided peace and certainty for her soul. Evenings were spent together eating home-made Palestinian dishes and talking until the early hours, usually with the extended family joining them and the laughter of children circulating in the air and reminding her of the optimism and hope they stayed strong for. The Eid celebrations that year were the best they had shared together and sang of the potential to come. The country nurtured her and provided everything she had been searching for. The empty hole inside her began to fill as she lived, belonging with her family, rooted in her faith that was a still a sapling longing to be fed.

She held the earth of the country in her ring. It was further proof that the country's history could create something beautiful. It reminded her that Josh had existed in her life. His whereabouts were unknown but everyone believed they knew how his story had ended. Jasmine couldn't escape the stories. One was told of a deal made with the Devil. The soldier swapped his life for the life of a dying man, the life of the father of the girl he loved. During the night in the ancient tombs, he had sold his soul and was granted twenty-four hours in this world before entering the next. He had spent those hours searching for his love but alas his soul was taken when the sun set the following evening.

Another was the story of the *Jinn* told around the fires at night-time, under the light of the moon. The *Jinn* had taken the form of an Israeli soldier, crossing paths with the Palestinian girl near the Dead Sea. It captivated her with its ancient stories told of the Holy Land, having lived there for many thousands of years and leading her to places humans could not go. It could take on whatever shape it wanted and if you were close enough to catch it change shape you would find its skin unnaturally cold to the touch. It was around her still, watching over her like a guardian, unaware that in fact it was held captive by her.

Another was a favourite when it came to the story of the Israeli soldier. He had been one of the best infiltrators they had ever trained. The Palestinian girl's family name had aroused suspicion as she entered the border. This super soldier was deployed to follow her and stage a seemingly innocuous meeting. He had then proceeded to cloud her heart with a combination of flattery and treachery as she digressed all of her secrets. Some say they still catch glimpses of him hiding behind the walls and in unlit corners of the border crossings, waiting for his next assignment.

But of them all, Jasmine's favourite was the story of the soldier who had set up an underground organisation fighting for humanity, just as his forefathers had done during war time Germany. He was the secret soldier who helped pregnant women through checkpoints so they could deliver their babies safely. He was the infiltrator who tirelessly recruited people to work together for a shared state and the collapse of the Wall. And why did the soldier do all of this? Because the one thing he loved more than the girl he couldn't have, was his country and it deserved a better future. Jasmine's skin tingled each time she heard it. She would ask for it to be told to her again and again. With her eyes closed she would imagine him being a part of the resistance.

When the days fell quiet, Jasmine roamed through the Holy City and searched for him in the certainty that the winding tunnels and passages carved beneath her hid him still. She heard his whispers in the breeze and it carried the scent of him in the night time air. She knew, when the time was right, she would find him again. Their story had only just begun.

ABOUT THE AUTHOR

Shereen Malherbe is a British Palestinian writer based in both the UK and the United Arab Emirates.

After visiting her father's home-land she was compelled to capture and preserve her family's history, which ultimately led to her first novel *Jasmine Falling*. Her aim in writing *Jasmine Falling* was to convey the hope that the Palestinian people exude with characters that represented positive aspects of both sides in the ongoing conflict that surrounds them.

Shereen Malherbe is also a writer for Muslimah Media Watch, a forum for critiquing the images of Muslim women in the media and pop culture.

If you would like to contact Shereen or see her other works you can find her at www.shereenmalherbe.com. You can also follow her on twitter @malherbegirl

54019534R00119

Made in the USA
Charleston, SC
22 March 2016